CHICAGO
LOOP

CHICAGO LOOP

BY
PAUL THEROUX

HAMISH HAMILTON
LONDON

HAMISH HAMILTON LTD

Published by the Penguin Group
27 Wrights Lane, London W8 5TZ, England
Viking Penguin Inc., 40 West 23rd Street, New York, New York 10010, USA
Penguin Books Australia Ltd, Ringwood, Victoria, Australia
Penguin Books Canada Ltd, 2801 John Street, Markham, Ontario, Canada L3R 1B4
Penguin Books (NZ) Ltd, 182–190 Wairau Road, Auckland 10, New Zealand

Penguin Books Ltd, Registered Offices: Harmondsworth, Middlesex, England

First published in Great Britain by Hamish Hamilton Ltd 1990

Copyright © Cape Cod Scriveners Co., 1990

Filmset in 12 on 14 pt Bembo

Printed in Great Britain by Richard Clay Ltd, Bungay, Suffolk.

A CIP catalogue record for this book is available from the British Library

ISBN 0-241-12949-4

'I've dreaded all the guilty dread
And done what they would fear to do.'
                    — *George Crabbe*, 'Frenzy'

Remorse — is Memory — awake
Her Parties all astir
A presence of Departed Acts
At window — and at Door
                        —*Emily Dickinson*

To Nic Roeg and Theresa Russell

I

ON West Adams, just inside the Loop, he was almost killed. A bus rose up as he glanced at the Sears Tower, he saw the driver's ugly and fearful face, he heard the hiss of the brakes. An instant later he thought: Why didn't I die?

Parker Jagoda had been wandering in the Loop all day. He told himself that he was just strolling. How could you call it procrastinating if you had no plans and nothing to do? It was a sunny day in early June, ninety-one degrees the billboards said in blinking lights. He hated the racket of the city but he felt strengthened by the heat and the crowds of people moving beneath the buildings.

He was always happier among strangers. Many people who knew him well wanted harm to come to him – and some wanted him dead. Former friends now simply envied him and would have delighted in his ruin, the way anyone weak is glad to see a powerful man disgraced. He knew this was true of his sour friends because he felt the distinct vibration of this envy: a low-frequency buzz that reached him sometimes from across a room, like fingers of heat, or slow poison; like a bad smell, like the drone of a dark light. And often when one of these people turned away the vibes seemed to come out of the back of their heads. Parker's apparent confidence, his energy, his family money – all of it – gave these people cramps. What could he do except avoid them? When he was friendly towards them, it was like a goad. His sharp humour made it worse. So he had no friends.

Now he was confused, though. Had he been loitering, waiting for that near accident with the bus? Seeing that he had survived it he decided that it was an omen, because it should have happened – he should have died.

He became decisive and headed for the piano bar on South Dearborn, where he knew there was a pretty stranger named Ewa sitting in front of a drink.

All day, believing that he was only bored, he had been seeing people from a distance, as though he happened to be visiting the planet, as though he had already died. Was it his age? He disliked being thirty-seven. He kept imagining what people might be doing, and he became like an alien – not a zombie, he knew that, because he was curious and energetic.

Today he was anonymous. He was unseen but he saw everything. Sadness had made him invisible and filled him with hateful humour. Wild puzzling jokes entered his mind, and he imagined the hurt, the bewilderment on people's faces if he had told them. It was a familiar feeling. Other people's happiness had always made him feel lonely.

Since leaving home he had been witnessing occurrences that no one else saw. He saw the truth. Why was the truth never apparent, always hidden, like a wicked secret? He saw a man wearing subtle make-up (eye-liner, highlights to define his cheekbones, something on his lips), and a woman with concealed tattoos: they showed like bruises through her tight summer-weight skirt, a rose on each buttock. A security man at LaSalle wore a wig – typical, this phoney cop with a woolly rug slipping sideways on his head. The man was happy, thinking he was fooling the world. Smudge-face was smiling, too. The tattooed woman was being a bitch.

2

Parker had been lingering at home in Evanston, and suddenly, as though hearing a signal in his head, he had run for the train. He missed the North Western train but caught a shabby El, full of cleaning ladies, heading home. He tried to guess which ones were Cambodians. Then he looked for omens at the window. He saw a young couple driving out of town in a new convertible – a Beemer like his own. Those two were lying to each other, but they were happy. He saw a family entering the premises of a travel agent, planning a vacation. They would almost certainly have a terrible time: it would rain, the flight would be bumpy, the people sitting behind them on the plane would put their feet on the armrests and whenever they got up to go to the toilet they would claw at the seatback in order to hoist themselves. That was hidden in the future, along with the people in the next room in their hotel – a man casually slapping a prostitute and quarrelling over money. Yet this travelling family was still ignorantly hopeful, just like the folks at Evanston he had seen greeting their weekend guests from Kenosha or somewhere else north – waiting at the station and eagerly welcoming the visitors with their much-too-heavy suit-cases. Everyone had plans for tomorrow. If they had seen Parker, he knew they would have said, 'We've got it and you haven't.'

He said to himself: People don't know they're awful. They think they're nice.

He wanted to shock them by telling them what they were.

That was when the train pulled into LaSalle in the Loop and he saw the security man in the badly-fitting wig. His purple uniform was a bad fit too; and his shoes were cracked and broken. It was a good thing a man like that didn't have a gun.

It was dark under the El at LaSalle, in this rich-poor,

lovely-crummy place, the financial district that was still grubby and real at the edges – the noisy Loop, where no one lived.

He knew exactly where he wanted to go, but he denied it. He walked slowly down Van Buren, under the El, liking the darkness and the hard shadows of the grid printed by the sunlight falling through the gaps in the steel. He passed the rosy granite of the Options Exchange, lingered near a bagel shop and looked up at the sudden structure of the new Cook County jail, the Metropolitan Detention Center, with its high window slits and twenty-five levels. It looked like a vault or a fort. He imagined being inside, behind a black slit, in the heat and boredom of a summer day. It would just be another way of living in Chicago, and not the worst.

'Spare any change for a guy?'

America was full of beggars these days and they frequented the best neighbourhoods, hung around the fanciest restaurants, made no apologies. This one was like the others: he looked respectable and dangerous, and Parker hated the man's insolence – this idea in the man's mind that he was just like Parker, really, only lacked money, had had a run of back luck, that string of lies. Parker wished he had the time to take the man aside and tell him how wrong he was and that he was dreadful.

He avoided the parking garage on Wells, where he usually put his car. He had left it in the lot at Davis Street, in Evanston. To be here in the Loop without it made him even more anonymous. It contributed to his Martian feeling. He walked around the corner and saw that it was almost four-thirty on the clock of the Board of Trade building. Parker did not look at his own expensive watch.

He then hurried – seemingly for no reason. Afterwards, he decided that he was hurrying to be killed, for a moment later on West Adams he was almost flattened by the Cicero bus.

Seeing a meaning in the way he had been spared, he walked quickly, with conviction, towards South Dearborn, and the woman waiting in the bar.

Ewa smiled as Parker entered the bar and headed towards her table. Parker knew there was relief and gratitude behind that smile, and he was amazed at her misguided certainty. He smiled, too, at the thought that she did not know him at all.

What she probably believed was what she had read in the ad in 'Personals' in the Chicago *Reader*.

> *If you are an attr., slender, health-conscious SWF (24–35) and if you like good food, fresh air, romantic evenings, and sharing great times, this SWM, 35, Loop exec., 5′11″, 160 lbs, financially and emotionally secure but lonely non-smoker would love to be part of your future. Write with photo and phone please to Box 91209.*

She replied in an oddly sloping left-handed script on a sheet of paper with a government-issue watermark. Her letter was all the more tender for being misspelt. She said she didn't want to get 'involved in a relationship'. She was 'real tired of bozos'. She couldn't spell commitment, but then no one could. She wrote 'your' meaning 'you're'. She said she had a mountain bike. In Chicago? 'No drugs', she said. She was lonely but she was cautious. No photo.

It was the sort of letter Parker imagined being written on a kitchen table under a glaring light. If you looked hard enough at the paper you'd find small crumbs and a coffee stain. He was prepared for a plain big-shouldered girl with the thighs of a major-league pitcher, who watched day-time TV in a large blue warm-up suit, and

5

had a slow sad way of eating. He had met many like that; the half-hour date. They were among the least trusting women who replied to personals.

But Ewa was a knock-out. She had long dark hair in one thick braid; she had clear skin and slanting Slavic eyes like a cat's, and a pouting Polish face and full lips. She was just under thirty, and though she had a good figure she dressed in heavy shapeless clothes like a day-labourer: a leather jacket and blue jeans and scuffed Reeboks, and she walked like a man, leaning forward and springing, with her hands jammed into her jacket pockets. Even today, in the nineties, she wore a sweatshirt.

He had been right about her caution, though. This was the fourth time he had seen her, and they had progressed no further than this bar. He had become cautious, too, as his feelings for her had grown tender; he might not even have kept today's date if there hadn't been that thing with the Cicero bus.

He said, 'I felt great this morning knowing that I was going to see you.'

'I was wondering whether you'd show,' she said, but she said it lightly.

'What would you have done if I hadn't?'

'What I always do,' she said, and sounded in-destructible.

Parker said, 'Did I ever tell you that one of my feet is a whole size bigger than the other? I'd like to show you this phenomenon sometime.'

From the way she smiled and lowered her head he knew that she suspected he was mocking her.

'I love to see guys with moustaches drinking beer,' he said. 'Look at that' – a man at a side table squeezed the suds from his moustache and frowned. 'Ever notice that men with sideburns always have them the wrong length? Like his – lopsided.'

Ewa laughed softly, liking him again.

He said, 'That's nice. I always hated it when my wife laughed at me, because she always used to laugh too hard. Much too hard, as though she meant something more by it. Know what I mean?'

That made Ewa check herself in a laugh, and she gave Parker another shy look that was puzzled and glum.

'Were you in Vietnam?' she asked.

'No! I've always been like this!' he said, surprising himself with his own joke. That made him affectionate. 'I really care about you,' he said. 'I love being with you.'

He hardly meant it, he was just talking again, but he needed her to accept it and believe him. If she had doubted him, he would have dropped her and gone away. He knew exactly where to go.

But Ewa accepted what he said, or seemed to – though they were only words. Her acceptance of them helped him wish himself into existence. He felt easy, just talking, drinking seltzer water with a squashed lime in it and watching her rattle the ice cubes in her junk drink – it was always Kahlua or Amaretto or another choker called Malibu. She seemed, so far, an unusual woman; she did not seem to need any more than words.

She said, 'I start believing you, and then I think – what's a dude like you need me for?' She made a face, because he didn't reply. She said, 'I'm boring.'

'No, you're not,' Parker said. 'Know why boring people are boring?'

Ewa shook her head and looked apprehensive, as though he was about to lecture her.

'They're boring because they think they're interesting.' She didn't get it, her eyes were still unfocused, trying to see the point.

'What about your wife?' she said. 'You mentioned your wife.'

7

He had forgotten that he had used the word, and it was wrong because S W M was the description he had used, not D W M. He was angry with himself for being so careless.

'It was a long time ago,' he said. 'She made a new friend. She didn't want me any more.'

'I know what that feels like,' Ewa said.

His anger left him, and he was glad to hear that new thing from her, because it was always the same conversation with her, and he was always thinking – but with slightly less interest as the days passed: *Who is she?*

He began to talk eagerly about her, insisting that she was not boring at all, and that he felt alive and hopeful when he was with her. At the same time, he was glancing around the piano bar and thinking: These people believe they are happy. They lead real lives, they are kind, they are harmless, they are simple. He envied them, then felt sorry for them, and pitied them. They did not know what was going to happen to them, and if they somehow found out – though that was impossible: only he knew such things – they would not be so jolly.

'You and your seltzer water,' Ewa said, in an affectionate way, like an old gently-joshing spouse. He had stopped talking and she was breaking the silence. She shrugged and said, 'I'm hungry.'

Parker called the waitress over and Ewa ordered, looking at the wall where the day's specials were chalked on a blackboard.

'Polish sausage in a roll, with mustard and ketchup. Cole slaw. Fries.'

'Anything more to drink?'

'White coffee,' Ewa said.

'I'll just have another glass of seltzer,' Parker said, and when the food came he smiled and said, 'That stuff's lethal.'

'Tell me about it.'

'I'd rather wait till you finish.'

He watched her eat – champing the sausage, snapping at the french fries, chewing the cole slaw, and when she was done she sipped her coffee and finished the last of the nuts and raisins from the bowl on the table.

'I guess you could call it a kind of passive suicide,' Parker said.

Ewa laughed at him, as though he had said something reckless; and Parker – in spite of himself – felt annoyed. Was she really so stupid after all?

'That sausage is made of mechanically recovered meat – they spin bones in a machine and collect a kind of muck of shredded meat, gristle, fat – and also bits of hair and bone. They grind it up, load it with nitrites, flavouring and preservatives and shove it into an edible condom to give it the right shape. The bread roll contains a slow poison called sodium-five to give a so-called fresh-baked flavour. Ketchup and mustard have artificial colouring: the poisonous synthetic kind made of coal tar. Your mayonnaise is total crap – it's all cholesterol, egg yolk, oil, thickeners, guar gum. And at this moment your blood is greasy – little blobs of grease in your blood stream – from the french fries.'

Ewa met his eye and belched loudly. 'You're full of shit.'

'If only you were, but it's worse than that. Guys grow breasts after eating meat like that. The hormones.'

Ewa straightened and said, 'I could use a few inches.'

'Why do you eat that crap?'

'I like the taste.'

'"Mouthfeel". It's a big reason. Crunch-crunch. It's organoleptic.'

Still Ewa was smiling.

'Those raisins you ate. You know they had mineral oil glaze on them?'

9

'That's the best part.'

'It causes anal seepage,' Parker said.

She stared at him. 'You're serious.'

He said nothing, and then he felt nauseated by what he had told her, and he wanted to go on, to sicken himself further and defy her.

'At least you didn't irritate the waiters.'

Ewa did not understand what he was saying.

'Eating in places like this. It's risky,' he said. 'If you get on the wrong side of the person serving you they're likely to spit in your soup or your coffee.'

Ewa glanced at her coffee cup, and her left hand closed, as though shrinking from picking it up.

'And if you really piss them off they take your bread roll or your bun and they go into the john and wipe it around the toilet seat and then put it delicately on your plate. You never know the difference. Ever see the wait-ress –'

'Cut it out,' Ewa said. She wasn't looking at Parker any more. She had turned away, and she looked sad and a bit lost – her arms folded against her loose sweatshirt. He knew he had hurt her: he had won. And so he found it easy to draw his chair nearer to her and take her hand. The hardness of her hand surprised him – her meaty palm, her callouses.

'I'm sorry,' he said.

She looked away grimly.

'I've got this thing about eating right. I had my first heart-attack when I was thirty.'

Only then did she turn to him – not with pity or sympathy, but with enough interest to encourage him.

'I almost died,' he said. But he did not think of the heart-attack because there was no heart-attack. He thought of the Cicero bus, rising up, looming over him and threatening to bury him. His face was creased in pain.

Ewa relented and said, 'I thought you were hassling me.'

'I wouldn't do that,' he said. 'But I guess I got carried away.'

'I'm not used to you yet,' she said.

'Yeah,' Parker said. 'I like that. I'll drink to that!' and he raised his glass of seltzer and sipped it and then kissed her. It was the first time they had ever kissed. She instinctively drew away, but she seemed pleased and embarrassed.

'I've been thinking about you all day in the office,' Parker said. 'Making plans. I figured we might go out for a change.'

She shrank almost imperceptibly. He knew she was uneasy. She clumsily seized on his mention of his office.

'How's that monster where you work?'

He smiled, slightly unsettled by her good memory.

Parker had told her that there was a weirdo he called The Monster in his office who went around stealing women's underwear. It was just a story he had told her so that he could pose the question: What do you suppose he does with the undies? He had no office like the one he described. There was no underwear-snatcher. Parker was an architect who had become a developer, renovating sites; his company, High Impact Properties, was on West Wacker.

But because she was watching him and wanted to change the subject Parker was prompt.

'You would not believe this guy,' he said. 'We know exactly what he's doing. He's apparently got this fabulous collection of women's panties in his desk drawer. God only knows what he does with it. Can you figure it out?'

Ewa said unhelpfully, 'I don't even want to think about it.'

'I guess he'll get caught eventually,' Parker said.

'You should turn him in. Make him famous. Even if he's not wacko it's still larceny.'

'Larceny – I love it,' Parker said. 'That says it all. Hey, he's harmless. And if he isn't they'll nail him when they know. When it all adds up. When he's got his ducks in a row.'

Ewa hesitated, then stammered and said, 'You seem a little edgy.'

'Me – edgy?'

He hated people saying such blunt things to him, confronting him, because such accusations usually provoked in him the very behaviour they questioned. Parker said he was very calm, and he wondered whether she believed him.

'So what about going out for a change?' he asked. 'Maybe to a nightclub.'

Ewa smirked at him and said, 'Can you see me in a nightclub?'

She meant dressed in her sweatshirt and sneakers.

'That's for starters,' Parker said. 'Maybe go someplace else afterwards.'

He knew from her face – her eyes alone – that she was not interested, and he was relieved.

'I wouldn't feel comfortable,' she said.

'It's okay,' he said, trying to conceal his relief: the tension that had just left him and allowed him to breathe freely. 'I'm not going to say another word about it. When we're ready we'll be ready.'

'Thanks for not nagging me,' she said, and touched his hand, then his cheek. The warmth of her fingers was like gratitude. 'God, I hate hassles.'

Was she thinking about what he'd said about her food? But she was over that. And he saw that by not insisting on the nightclub, by being deferential, he had made her trust him. Just like that, she would cling, more strongly than if she had been in love with him and desired him, because he was so easy and did not insist.

It has to be someone else, Parker thought, and looked at his watch. Only six-thirty: and yet he knew another woman was getting dressed and would be waiting – knew her name, knew her height and weight. She was just now looking in a mirror at her face, but she was thinking of him. She too was eager and hopeful, because they had never met.

He was suddenly impatient for Ewa to go. He stood up, so that she would do the same. He told her how much he wanted to see her again. They were just simple words – only human noises – but Ewa smiled and said, 'I like you' with the same emphatic conviction that women he knew usually reserved for love or desire.

He wanted to say that he liked being with her because she required nothing of him, and because she believed him. But he knew that if he told her how little he wanted of her she would drop him altogether, or she would panic, out of suspicion and fear, the way some women did.

'I have to go,' she said.

Where did she go? He didn't ask.

'You're not the nosy type, are you?' she said.

'I'm the happy type,' Parker said, and he felt happy now, seeing her gather up her bag and shove her chair back into place against the table.

'Save a little for me,' Ewa said. In that instant, and for the first time, she sounded lonely.

'Trust me,' Parker said.

She looked hopeful, grateful, and they almost kissed again. She touched his lips with her fingers, where the kiss would have gone, and then she seemed to be listening to the piano. It was playing 'Time After Time' and Parker knew she was thinking of the lovely words.

Parker took her hand, and his eagerness for her to go and leave him, the consoling way he spoke to her, reassured her and made her linger.

He said, 'I have room in my life for you. But do you have room in your life for me?'

The look she gave him then – just a subtle widening of her eyes – said everything. There was an empty space in her life, the sort of airless gap that was suffocating, and he saw her alone in her lonely room. She listened to sad songs and grew sadder.

'We're going to be fine,' he said.

The way she glanced around convinced him that she was thinking of herself and him together. To such a solitary woman the word *we* had power and beauty. He was almost afraid for her, afraid of his power over her. He was glad to see her go, for now.

He still had time to walk the mile and a half to Felix's, the bar on North Rush where the woman named Sharon (SWF, 5′4″, 108 lbs, 'streaky blonde') was probably waiting. It was their first meeting, and so she would either be on time or else wouldn't show at all.

The *Reader* personal ad she had answered had said,

Successful, strong, unusual, generous SWM, 35, own business, seeking open-minded fun-loving fem. for dates, companionship, and future. Send note, photo, phone no. to Box 58362.

The note was brief, in green ink, but the photo would have been enough: there was recklessnes in her face. She was darkly tanned, with short bright hair, and the top buttons on her blouse undone. She smiled like someone looking for a job, and on the phone – yes, she knew Felix's – she had an odd, hungry, swallowing way of speaking. Friday was fine, and at the time – this was last week – Parker wondered whether he would show up.

14

Yet here he was pushing through the crowd at Felix's and looking for Sharon's hair. She was in a corner, being pestered by a man who vanished as soon as Parker spoke.

She said, 'You're just the way I imagined you.'

They had a drink. She asked for a vodka, calling it a Stoly, and he had seltzer again.

'I thought we might go to a nightclub,' he said, 'and then somewhere else afterwards.'

He felt he was being absolutely impartial. They were no more than words. If a woman acted on them she had to take the consequences. It was not like opening a door and saying 'Come on in'; it was unlocking the door, and telling the woman it was unlocked. It was for her to decide whether she wanted to find out what was on the other side of the door.

Sharon was grinning tipsily. 'You mean a nightspot or a nightclub?'

'Is there a difference?'

'You eat in one and you drink in the other, but I don't know which is which,' she said. 'I mean, I've never been in one long enough to find out.'

On the phone, in their first conversation, she had said, *What do you mean 'unusual'? What do you mean 'generous'?* And he had said, *I think I mean the same thing that you do*, and she had laughed in a wicked way.

'I mean, hit 'em and quit 'em – that's what usually happens.'

There was something about her laugh that made Parker think that she knew exactly what she was doing. It was laughter echoing wide experience.

'What have you been doing all day?'

'Just bumming,' Sharon said. She had small breasts and tiny hands and froggy-lidded eyes, and when there was that shriek in her laugh he saw that her teeth were large and even. 'Hanging out, because of the heat.'

15

'Are you alone?'

She laughed hard and he saw those teeth again.

'You're about the billionth guy today that's asked me that.'

She spoke easily and unaffectedly, as though they were old friends. But Parker felt it was something else — she was always talking to strangers. She was still talking.

'I came in at noon to chill out,' she said. 'I'm just walking in and there's about a million guys at the bar, so I comes over here and sits down, and people start sending drinks over to me, like fifty at a time. Then they're all hitting on me. What is it with these guys? I would've left but it's boiling hot outside, about two hundred degrees, practically melting the street, and they're, like, talking about a drought, don't water the lawn, don't take a bath. About five hundred times a day they're announcing it on the radio. Anyway, I left, because they were hitting on me —'

He wanted her to stop talking. 'What about that night-club?' he said.

Sharon had a small girl's way of twisting her lips and making an exaggerated face before she spoke, to demonstrate that she was thinking it over.

'I'd have to change first,' she said.

'We can change after,' he said.

She looked sharply up at him. 'What is this, one of these twenty-four hour gigs?'

He raised his hands slightly and smiled and said, 'It's entirely up to you.'

'Yeah,' she said, and made that small girl's face again.

She could have said no. She could have said anything. He had not forced her; just the way he had lifted his hands had shown her she was in charge. And so she would have to take the consequences. She really was in charge. Having agreed to meet — having agreed to go —

she was admitting that she knew him. She had been around strange men before – that was obvious. Perhaps, Parker thought, she knew him better than he knew himself, which imposed an even greater responsibility on her.

Getting in the taxi she said, 'Hey I like your shoes.'

'They help my feet breathe,' he said.

Sharon didn't laugh. She looked more alarmed by his remark than if he had said something wild.

'Both of my feet are exactly the same size,' he said. 'That's very rare.'

The alarm was still on her face, and she turned away from him when she spoke again.

'The way I look at it is, they go together. If a guy's unusual he's got to be generous.'

The taxi driver laughed, and both Parker and Sharon looked up. But this black man was laughing at a miniature portable TV set that was propped up on the front seat beside him, playing 'The Dating Game'.

2

ENTERING the cavernous restaurant with Sharon, Parker passed the air-conditioner, which made the same sound as an oil-burner, but howling much louder, and from its dusty vent in the wall it sent out this noise and filled the room with a stinking chill. The cool air seemed to preserve and heighten the smell of rotting carpets, spices, stale food, clammy plaster and dead insects.

The place was called Scheherazade, it was nearly empty, but when Parker commented on this, the waiter said, 'We are busy later. It is too early to eat.' It was as though he was reproaching Parker – and was that an accent or did he have food in his mouth?

Sharon looked around at the paintings of mosques and minarets, the carpets hanging like paintings, the brass lanterns, the camel saddles and bells and candlesticks, and – for some reason – fishnets with cork floats tangled in them.

'I bet they have great food here,' Sharon said.

Was she joking? She was still wearing her sunglasses, so Parker couldn't tell.

'I love Chinese food. Slurp-crunch, slurp-crunch.'

Her glasses flashed as she glanced around at the paintings and the brassware. 'I'd like to travel sometime,' she said. 'Go to Europe. Paris. Places like that.'

'Have you ever been out of Chicago?'

'The Yucatán. Once. I'd rather not talk about it.'

Parker shrugged, but he wanted to know.

'Never go anywhere with an alcoholic,' she said. 'They just bring you down.'

Parker decided that it was part of her stupidity that she was serious in everything she said.

She was still talking, but she bored him already in the way she paused repeatedly in her monologue. She made him impatient, and yet her body was small and interesting. He knew that she would understand him only when he took hold of her. Whether she would allow it was another matter; the choice was hers.

Just then, a woman entered the restaurant swiftly, carrying a small black overnight bag. She was a bit breathless, she was pale, she wore a tee-shirt and blue jeans. The man at the door chatted to her. All this Parker saw reflected in the mirror by the entrance, and while he was still concentrating on her she vanished.

The waiter approached. There was something foreign in the way he moved, in the flexing of his fingers, in the way he held his head – an accent in his body. He handed over a thick menu, with a heavy tassel swinging from its spine. But Parker said they weren't hungry and he ordered drinks instead. A vodka for Sharon, a glass of seltzer for himself.

Interrupted in her story about the alcoholic, Sharon began eating from the bowl of dry roasted chickpeas on the table.

'They've got salt on them,' Parker said. 'That bowl alone represents serious water retention.'

She made a face at him, and then began to laugh very hard, as though Parker had told a terrific joke. When her laughter ended, she simply stopped. She hadn't really thought that anything was funny; she became serious again and said, 'I eat what I want.'

Music – of flutes and drums, with a clatter of a tambour-
ine – came from a speaker in the corner, and a sliding
light found a woman in a flimsy red dress entering the
room on tiptoe and dancing forward. It was the pale
young woman he had seen earlier carrying the black bag
and talking shyly with the Arab at the entrance. But she
was changed, and the transformation shocked and disgusted Parker.

'That's what I told this guy,' Sharon said – which guy?
– ' "I eat what I want." '

The dancer affected a slinky way of moving, and she
shook her hips in a rapid belly-dancer's motion, with a
speed and direction that would have mixed a gallon of
paint. There was something heartless and mechanical in
it, in just that motion, the blur of her gauzy red skirt, the
whirling of her arms, that made her seem not simply
whorish but sinister and dangerous.

'She's probably from Skokie,' Sharon said. 'I know,
because I'm from Skokie. She's dying to be made.'

The remark came so abruptly Parker wondered whether
Sharon was quick-witted, but he decided no – she was
probably just vicious. And what did she care? She was still
talking about the man, her story mingling with the music.

'He bought me about a hundred drinks and then we
got into his car. It was huge, about fifty feet long, like
one of these stretch limos. And people are looking at me
– who is she? I could almost hear them. And we rode for
about nine hundred miles. I mean, this place he lived in
was way past O'Hare –'

The dancer could have been from Skokie. She wasn't
Arab, she wasn't very young, she was skinny. She wore
bracelets and anklets, she was barefoot, she struck little
cymbals in her fingers. She knew exactly what she was
doing. She came near the table, she did not move her
head, she fixed Parker with her snake-charmer's snare –

her mascara was sticky – and she shook her frantic pelvis at him. She didn't smile, she seemed very sure of herself, thinking *I push this at you and you want to snatch it.* He hated her and he hated being a man.

'It's a nice costume,' Sharon said. 'Them are expensive, them are imported. You can tell.'

She seemed to want it, and if she had she would put it on and do the same. She had done the same with the man who had taken her beyond O'Hare in his big car.

'When we got to his place and he started hitting on me I said, "Cut it out" but did he listen? "Then what did you come here for?" I just looks at him. I says, "I thought you respected me."'

Parker laughed angrily at that, looking past Sharon to the skinny pale woman jiggling her hips. The crass music shattered in the air. Parker was still laughing as Sharon continued her story, and he realized that the music had killed the cruelty in his laughter: all she probably saw was his open mouth.

'We're in this room. There's a bed – it's about fifty feet wide. There's a carpet so thick I'm practically up to my waist in it. He pours me a drink – this humungous glass, it takes like a whole bottle of Stoly to fill it, and all the while he's sort of following me around –'

'And you didn't have any idea what he wanted?' Parker said.

The belly-dancer was also prowling now, shimmying as she walked, crooking her arms, moving her fingers and shoulders. She approached some men at another table. She pursed her lips, reddening them; she had bangles on her biceps; she glared at the men. Her costume had been designed to excite men, and yet each time a man leaned forward she drew away. She was too quick for anyone to caress her, but not quick enough to avoid being caught and hurt.

21

Sharon said, 'He started to get smart with me. You know – make remarks. He was on my case. Still hitting on me.'

'You were standing there in his room at night with your hair like that and a drink in your hand.'

'So what?' Sharon said. It was the first sign of her defiance. Then she smiled and looked triumphant. 'He was a wimp. I told him to take me home. Anyway, he did.'

The belly-dancer circled towards them again and a man stuffed a five-dollar bill into the waistband of her gauzy skirt, and another one tucked some money into her bra. The dollars showed darkly against her skin, the points of their corners. She was near Parker as she invited him to look at her. Parker gave her such a look of menace – so hateful and corrosive – that she seemed to shudder as she danced away, and Parker turned back to Sharon, who was obviously still thinking about that man she had mocked.

The dancer had gone, but the music was still playing as Parker said, 'I was in a fraternity at Northwestern. Every Saturday night a guy used to take a different girl there up the stairs and into his room. We'd be watching from the kitchen. We didn't have dates, and we were so envious of this guy. After about an hour, and sometimes more, the girl would come out of the room, looking pale and sort of dreamy and rumpled, and the guy behind her just staring straight ahead to take her home. People get a certain look in their eye after they've really had it – a kind of vacant, empty look, like they've been punctured. Off they'd go. The following week it would be someone else, the same look afterwards.'

'Some guys have the knack,' Sharon said. 'But some chicks are looking for it.'

'That's what we tried to find out,' Parker said. 'So one

Saturday night we put a tape recorder under the bed in his room. Did I mention he was Polish? But that's not important. He took a girl up. They always looked so innocent. After an hour or so they left, and she had that look but even more so, glittering from sex, and dazed, because she'd had it over and over – her eyes were bright and exhausted, like she had a fever.'

'What about the tape recorder?'

'As soon as they had gone we sneaked in and retrieved it, and we took it into the attic to play the tape. It was really odd. There were no voices on it at first. Then we heard the sound of sighs and grunts and whispers. The girl was being held very hard – I imagined her arm twisted behind her back, because I heard the guy say, "Take off your clothes and don't bother to scream, be-cause if you do I'll snap your arms in half, I'll pinch your head off" – and the girl whimpered – "I'll cut your face so bad no one will look at you." Then there were no more voices. The woman didn't say yes, she simply sighed harshly, like someone who's been burned, sort of surprise and shock, a sigh of dismay.'

'Maybe he tied her up,' Sharon said hopefully.

'Maybe very tight,' Parker said. 'We heard the bed. We heard the struggle, and the breathing. It went on for a long time, and so did the silences. Then the gasps again, animal noises. After a long time we heard the door slam and it was over.'

Sharon was staring at Parker, her lips slightly parted – was that a smile? She took his hand. Her fingers were soft and damp and very small. She dragged his hand under-neath the table, across her thighs, made him fumble with the hem of her skirt.

'Touch me,' she said, and she parted her legs and helped him.

It was as though he were stroking the opening of a large

hot wound, a stabbing that had just happened, and it took a moment for him to be convinced that he was not hurting her, that she was not bleeding.

'Do you want to go?' he asked.

'What a question.'

'Answer it,' he said, and he inquired with his hand too.

Sharon smiled again, she tugged his hand and lifted it and licked the wetness from his fingers.

He was afraid for her. He excused himself and went to the men's room in order to stall. He did not want to appear to be loitering there, and so he left and lingered in the entry-way, where there was a mirror. He saw at his feet the black overnight bag and – near the kitchen – the belly-dancer in her street clothes, the tee-shirt and blue jeans.

He told himself that he was taking the bag to do the woman a favour. She did not know how dangerous it was to wear those clothes; he might be saving her life. He found Sharon in the darkness of the restaurant and she stood up, eager to leave.

'South Blue Island Avenue, at Throop,' she told the taxi driver, and, seeing the bag in Parker's hand, 'What's that?'

'Old clothes,' he said. It came out so quickly she didn't question it further.

'God, I'm hot,' she said, turning to him.

He had never heard a woman say that without thinking that she meant something else: a clumsy and crude innuendo.

Her eyes were still on him. 'Unusual, generous,' she said, as though uttering a formula that somehow described their relationship, but her tone was tentative, she was trying the words out on him to see whether he would deny them.

'That's the first time I ever put a personal ad in the paper,' he said.

'That's the first time I ever answered one of them.'

They knew they were both lying and the lie reassured him and made him feel a conspiratorial bond with her.

'I've got rules,' she said. 'You want to know my rules?'

Parker was thinking: She knows everything. She wants this to happen. She is making this happen.

'No drugs,' she said. 'No weapons. No other people.'

She was facing him, with that defiance in her eyes that he had seen earlier.

'No animals,' she said.

Then she smiled at him.

'No other animals,' she said.

The city lights dazzled him in the taxi, which was racing down Blue Island Avenue towards Sharon's apartment – 'Don't expect much,' she said, but she was smiling and he thought: *She is cooperating*.

He wanted to know why she was smiling. *I am doing nothing except letting this happen*, he told himself.

At her building he noticed two things about her: that she was drunk, and that she had a slight limp. She was not self-conscious enough to realize that she lived in a desperate neighbourhood, and he was glad she didn't seem to know how miserable this building was. He had a strong sense that she didn't know who he was. He was a man, no more than that; like the man in her story, like the man in his – more now like the men in those stories than the man who had placed the personal ad in the *Reader*. Anyway, that was just a joke now, and they couldn't mention it again because they had both lied about it.

On the stairs she said several times, 'So you're going to stay awhile?'

He realized that she was talking about the overnight bag that he had taken from the restaurant. He hoped it was not empty – it felt so light.

She was undoing the locks on her door – three different locks – and then she pushed the door open. The day's heat, from sun-up until dusk, like a harvest of those hours of light, was contained in the room – thin stale heat and the smell of coffee, the hum of a refrigerator, the sound of the street filtered through brick and glass, a cheap clock – its uncertain tick-tock; and all at once – the apartment was that small.

'Drink?' she said.

'I've had enough,' he said. He had had nothing.

'I haven't,' she said. She sat among Mexican souvenirs – painted clay candlesticks, a day-glo pinata, a blue straw mat at her feet.

She poured herself a glass of tequila, and he sat and waited for her to drink it. A moment later the glass was empty. How had she drunk it so quickly? Time seemed to pass in spasms. Why was it that people guzzled poisons: fats, salts, oils, egg yolks, chemicals and forbidden colourings. It was a way of being naughty, but did they know they were killing themselves? At some point Sharon said, *Want to go next door?* She meant the bedroom, he knew that, but why didn't she say so?

Instead of replying, he opened the overnight bag. There was a flash of red, a glitter of gold thread shot through the fabric, a motion of loose fringes – the belly-dancer's costume. It was so small without a human body inside it.

'What's that?' She smiled at the brightness and reached for it and held it up. It was gauzy, he could see her face through it.

'Want to put it on?'

She laughed at him. 'I haven't heard that in a long time. "Want to put it on?"' She said it as though there was nothing she wanted more than to put it on.

She began to undress, right there in front of him. He

had always hated seeing a woman undressing, all the awkward stretching and stooping postures, and she was more ungainly than many woman he had seen. She bent and went round-shouldered and hung her head, and her clothes wrinkled and shrivelled: what had contained her flesh was no more than a slight tissue of shapeless crumpled cloth. You could hold all her clothes in your hand and squeeze them into a ball and stuff them into your pocket and walk away.

'Please, not here,' he said.

She had been stooping – looking ducklike and flat-footed as she stepped out of her skirt – and then she picked up the skirt, and gathered the costume, and she was like a woman in a warehouse going from room to room with an armful of wrinkled clothes.

Her limping, slightly sideways way of walking gave him two opposing thoughts. I could push her over, was one; and the other: I could protect her. But why – if she was so weak – had she invited him there? Why had she said *Touch me* and dragged his hand down, why had she answered that provocative ad in the *Reader*? He had tried to warn her with his story about the fraternity house, but it had only aroused her. *Touch me*.

He had already begun to resent her, because just by being there his whole life was going to change. He felt that. He also felt that he had no idea what was going to happen next. He had agreed to be with her. She was in charge. Everything that happened in these small rooms was her responsibility now: he was merely an instrument, doing what she asked. She had invited him.

You're just the way I imagined you, she had said. She knew exactly what she was doing.

'Bye now,' she said. She was leaving the room, and it was as though she was leaving for good.

Parker thought: I could be free. I can go – just leave

this place and go home, and it will be over. I would never see her again. All she knows is my box number. He seriously wondered why he was sitting there, and he summoned all his will to leave, and stood up to get to the door.

'In here,' she said, from the next room, in a wicked-innocent voice, and in that moment – for making him stay – he hated her.

She stepped towards him when he entered the room, and that step – the movement of her slender leg – travelled through her body in a slow and sinuous ripple.

She wore a red bra, the gauzy veil-like shawl and filmy pantaloons. She was slightly bigger and fleshier than the belly-dancer had been, and so she looked more obvious and eager. She was beckoning, but the only sound was the simple chiming of her silver bracelets.

The fear in Parker was like a twisting in his throat that prevented him from pleading for her to stop – for her own good, and so that he could breathe.

She was smiling and swaying, moving artlessly, and that was worse, because she was unable to conceal her intention. He knew she wanted to trick him and rouse the destructive fool within him. But if she succeeded – and she was trying it knowingly – she would have to deal with the consequences. It was entirely her responsibility.

Her hips moved in a slow circle as she padded towards him and he had just a glimpse of her dirty footsoles. There was a logic in her body – instinct and expression and intention, not eloquent but plainly selfish and demanding, as her hips revolved and beckoned, as though reeling him in. Her upper body and her head remained erect and proper.

The whole effect would have been Arab and enigmatic if it were not for her reckless face. It was not the heavy-lidded and pinch-nosed mask of the black-haired woman at

Scheherazade. It was the face of a devilish little coquette. Didn't she know that she was dangerous, tempting him this way, provoking him, teasing him, the way she probably had that man in Yucatán that she had ended up calling a wimp. It all showed in her eyes and mouth, her greed, her stupid cunning, like those little girls — nieces, the children of friends, the urchins in parks, the ones who put their small chubby fingers on a snake and said *Look at me*.

'Like my dress?' she said.

Parker imagined himself saying, *Be very careful or you'll get hurt. You think you can control me, but if you go too far you'll regret it and you'll never get back —*

He hated this tone of warning and moralizing. Even saying it silently in his mind exasperated him. Anyway, she knew this — it was because she knew it that she was dancing around him.

'Stop it,' he said, because that short warning was at the centre of all his anxious moralizing.

Seeing him very serious made her smile, and she danced faster, seeming to get the hang of it. There was a thrill in her that was the more spirited for the way he frowned at her. In just that same way he had frowned at the food that disgusted him — meat and fat and salt and the colouring that came from coal tar.

He snatched at her, missed, and she laughed seeing him falter and almost topple over. He recovered his balance and turned quickly. She was still dancing. He finally stopped her by shoving her hard against the wall — upsetting a chair, and there was dried knuckle of chewing gum stuck to its underside — and holding her arms.

Her bright eyes fastened on him and didn't blink. 'What are you going to do to me?'

He could not speak. He did not know. He wanted her to break free of his grasp, but she hardly struggled. She allowed him to hold on, and she leaned into him, grazing him with her breasts as she spoke again.

'You're hurting my wrists,' she said. It was not a complaint, more a murmur of amazement, and she parted her lips when he gripped her harder.

Still Parker held her against the wall – he loosened his grip to give himself a rest, and yet she didn't move; she remained in the same trapped posture.

'You could do anything to me,' she said, in a curious and wondering way, as though fascinated by the word *anything* and trying to give it a more specific meaning. 'I can't move. You're a billion times stronger than me.'

'Leave me alone,' he said. *Leave me alone!* Even as he said it he saw the absurdity of his muttering that, as though it were she holding him against the wall.

But it seemed that way – as though she had him cornered, that was how he felt. And when she laughed she sounded strong. He had no words left to reply to her – he stuttered and then slapped her clumsily.

'Didn't hurt,' she said, in her little teasing voice.

He took her by the wrists again as she came nearer seeming to offer them. They were pale white and pink where he had squeezed before, and her damp face was lighted with eager expectation. He drew her hands against her body, pushing her breasts together, tangling her fingers in the silk and red fringes of the belly-dancer's costume.

Her eyes mocked him – she saw his indecision: he did not know what to do. He still wanted her to break free. He was not holding her tightly – why didn't she struggle? She was cooperating, she was trying to help him.

'You better not tie me up,' she said.

And that face. She spoke the words just as a child would have, he thought – she didn't mean it, she was helping him to think, she was making a suggestion.

She lost her balance and Parker righted the chair he had tipped over. He guided her into it, pretending to be rough but at the same time fearful of hurting her. She smiled and reached behind her, as though to show him how she should be tied. That gesture – her arms drawn back – forced her face and breasts forward. She watched him closely – all this time with the same excitement, the same bright impudent eyes.

He obeyed. He used the flimsy clothes she had taken off and he knotted them on her wrists and ankles. He was doing as he had been ordered. He had been obeying her ever since she'd grasped his hand at Scheherazade and said *Touch me*. Then he had touched her hot wet wound and his fingers sank into her.

'Not too hard,' she said.

He took this to mean *harder*, and obeyed. She stiffened and tried to get free.

She groaned, the sound rising from deep in her throat – he could not translate it as either pain or pleasure. She remained motionless as she uttered it again. There was just that sound, and her still body in the belly-dancer's costume.

Now Parker stood over her. He did not know how to begin, and he felt that he was the helpless one, that she was controlling him – that he was the one tied up and immovable.

Her small upturned face was like a child's again, at the level of his waist. Her eyes had not left him, they were still smiling at his confusion.

'You better not bite me.'

Only then did he drop to his knees. She tilted her head back and moved her lips to receive his kiss. But he surprised her – that same groan came from her throat – as he buried his face in the skin and bones of her neck, and with the perfume of her soft breasts warming his face, he bared his teeth and began.

3

H E lay in bed inert, as though under a pile of broken things – a clutter of dark fragments holding his head down in sleep that was all darkness and disorder.

Then he woke to a loud crick-cracking like narrow bones breaking, crushed in old wicker, and a flutter like flags whipping in a stiff breeze. It was fire. He raised himself and saw its garishness, the vulgar colour of flames, filling the television screen at the end of the bed.

His own bed: he was home, he was safe, rising through the still pool of sleep, and surfacing – bright day on the white curtains. His memory sank and drowned in all that sunlight.

'– *a helicopter picture of forest fires that are burning out of control and devastating Yellowstone National Park – an ecological tragedy, say experts. Is there any hope, or is it already too late to save the park from virtual extinction?'*

'Hey, it's never too late, Bryant,' Parker said in a clear voice.

And Barbara sat up and laughed.

'On the other hand, let's cancel our trip to Yellowstone, honey. The whole place looks like a barbecue pit.'

'You're so cruel,' Barbara said, but she was still laughing.

'*I'm Bryant Gumbel and this is "Today", Tuesday, June*

seventh, nineteen-eighty-eight. First the news with John Palmer. John?'

'*Thank you, Bryant —*'

Parker looked at the screen again: the fire was still burning, and firemen with sooty faces were dragging hoses through the smoke.

'They love it,' he said.

Barbara threw off the sheet and swung her legs off the bed.

'I've never seen a woman fireman,' Parker said. 'I've never seen a woman working at a shoe-shine stand, or a woman sea-captain.' And he reached down and snatched Barbara's long-haired wig from the floor and crammed it on his head. Turning to Barbara he said, 'Furl the mainsail, you faggots!'

'I hear the baby,' Barbara said.

'But the best haircut I ever had was from that woman barber over on Erie, behind the Veterans' Hospital. No questions, and she used her fingertips, and she knew how to give a shave with a cut-throat razor.'

Parker was talking seriously, but still wearing the silky-haired wig, and Barbara laughed at the absurdity of it.

'You're too much,' she said, leaving the bedroom.

'*— and Mrs Minnette Frayne of Hurlburt, Kentucky, is one hundred years old today. Dorothy Betts of Madison in the great state of Wisconsin is one hundred and two. Bless her. Happy birthday to them, and Happy fiftieth birthday to the Cleveland Institute of Food Science who sent me this scrumptious pound cake — but it weighs about ten pounds, and I'm going to eat the whole thing after the show. Now let's check the act —*'

Barbara entered the room, holding the baby, and Parker was struck by how shapeless and toylike he was.

'Take the wig off, darling. You'll freak him out.'

But Parker kept it on and said, 'Hello, Poopoo, come to Daddy.'

Seeing him, the baby crooked his tiny fingers and something within his small face twisted and squashed its mouth, and with a bitter energy the child began to cry. Parker slipped the wig off and drew Barbara near to him. He never felt closer to her than when she was holding him, with the baby whimpering softly beside her, the three of them together in bed.

'You weren't supposed to see that,' Barbara said.

She took the wig from the pillow and tossed it on to a chair, where it sprawled grotesquely – it was something worse than disorder: a wig on its own always suggested violence, Parker felt.

'*– that if the polls are correct the vice-president has already been very badly hurt by the allegations –*'

Barbara said, 'I bought it for Friday,' and she let this sink in. 'Did you forget?'

It was a moment before Parker understood what she meant, and then he remembered the arrangement they had made months ago, Barbara saying, *As soon as we can start using baby-sitters for little Eddie we'll have a real date.*

'I didn't forget,' he said. 'But why did you leave it lying around the bedroom?'

'Don't scold. You said you probably wouldn't be home last night,' Barbara said. 'I was surprised when you crawled into bed. What was it – one-thirty? two?'

'Oh, yeah. I finished early.' Finished *what*? His mind was a blank. 'I got a train. I wanted to wake up with you and Eddie.'

The baby was sucking at the hem of the flower-patterned pillow case.

'I'm glad you did,' Barbara said. 'And just to prove it I'm going to bring you breakfast in bed.' She lifted the baby and stood up and moving forward she tripped over Parker's shoes. She swore softly. 'New shoes.'

'Yeah. So my feet can breathe.'

'Daddy's such a silly man,' Barbara said to the baby as she left.

There was a moustached man on the television screen. He wore a rumpled army uniform and was speaking angrily to a reporter. And then there were scenes of a loud smoking battle in what Parker guessed was Central America.

'– repeated incursions over the border –'

But much of the interview was drowned in gunfire and shouting and in the croaking of helicopter gunships. A wounded man in a stretcher, a bloody bandage around his leg, was bumped across a field towards a jeep by men who moved like pallbearers in a hurry.

'What's that?' Barbara said, but didn't wait for an answer. She was holding a tray: Parker's breakfast. It was a cup of Postum, oat-bran porridge, a banana and a dish of sliced apples.

'The thing is,' Parker said, starting to smile, 'to get all those poisons out of your body. See, this is all clean-burning. Soluble fibre.'

'First give me a kiss,' Barbara said.

But Parker had sat up straight and with unexpected urgency was fumbling with the remote switch.

'What are you trying to do?'

'This goddamned thing –'

'Back in a moment. This is "Today" –'

'We don't want to see this,' Parker said angrily, and in the same instant the screen went black just as the Chicago skyline and the newscaster on 'Dateline Chicago' appeared.

'You shouldn't have done that, darling.'

'He was staring at us,' Parker said.

Barbara laughed and said, 'It's the Chicago news and weather!'

'Don't worry,' Parker said, 'it's going to be another beautiful day.'

She mentioned the weather again on the way to Davis Street station. She was a lovely woman, but when she repeated something – and this was her third time on the weather – her face became fixed and insistent, an older expression hardening within it. Parker often looked at her photographs and thought: If anyone heard her speaking in that smug North Shore honk they wouldn't think she was so lovely.

'If there's rain the traffic will be terrible,' Barbara said.

'It won't rain. That's a promise. Is this guy supposed to be good?'

'Jakes is fantastic, and this Mapplethorpe exhibit is full of great stuff. It's exciting –'

That was another thing about her: when she was driving she hardly seemed aware of what she was saying, and she seldom listened.

It was only when she was inattentive that she used words like 'fantastic' and 'exciting'.

'As long as there's an exhibition to go to – that's the main thing,' Parker said.

'And we're having a drink afterwards with him,' Barbara said. 'He's supposed to be very big on leather.'

'As long as he meets us,' Parker said. 'That's what really matters.'

At the red light Barbara said, 'I can't tell whether you're mocking or not.'

'I'm not mocking,' Parker said. 'It's something to look forward to. What about tomorrow night?'

'I'm taking the baby to my mother's.'

'And Friday I have a date.'

'You bet.' And she drew up at Evanston Station.

When he went to kiss her she moved her head aside and offered him her cheek, like a vague acquaintance saying goodbye. You had to remember that – how she didn't like her lipstick smudged, how hugging her made

36

her complain that you were creasing her blouse, how she shrank when she was touched. And those quirks isolated her and made her beautiful to look at. She had clear blue eyes and a sensual mouth and short hair spiked brown and blonde.

Parker made for the gate, waved the newspaper seller aside, and on the train he struck up a conversation with the man next to him. It was a tiny man of sixty or so, who put his *Tribune* down and said he had been up since four that morning, tending his roses in the greenhouse, something he always did before catching his train. He was in advertising, he said, but he preferred to talk about rose-growing.

'I'm also interested in flowers,' Parker said. 'I've got a huge garden. I'm always weeding and spraying. I love seeing things grow – the progress from day to day.'

'My wife helps me,' the man said. 'Does yours?'

'I'm a widower,' Parker said.

The man looked shocked and touched his face, as though in terror. 'I'm sorry –'

'She was very ill. It was one of these merciful releases.'

The man talked about his own health after that, and he did not ask where Parker worked until they were at the Loop.

'Garment Workers' Union,' Parker said. 'I'm their special counsel. I do most of their legal work.'

'Good for you. My father was in that union,' the man said, in the same solemn and reflective tone he would have used for speaking about a religion. It was as though, Parker thought, the mention of the union stirred many memories – of his father, of the past, of hard times. The man then became vague and lost his smile in thought, and after he had gone Parker asked himself why he lied to such an insignificant man, and concluded: Because he was insignificant. The truth was for those few who really mattered.

37

The first thing he did at the office was to call Ewa. He was used to getting her answering machine, and when he heard her voice it took him a few seconds to reply, wondering whether it was a tape running.

'Hi,' he said. 'It's me. I'm free tomorrow night.'

She did not answer at once. He knew she was hesitating – that she could not understand his interest in her.

'I have to see you.'

'Okay,' she said, seeming somewhat bewildered and yet persuaded by the very force of his force. 'Same place?'

'No. Let's try somewhere else,' Parker said. 'I don't want to get into a rut.'

He worked after that. There was a time when he would have spent the day sketching buildings – not just the structure but the details of every door and window frame, every lock and shelf and ornament. One of the sets of plans framed on Parker's walls was that of the house the philosopher Wittgenstein had designed for his sister in which he had done just that thing – taken responsibility for every detail. These days – today for example – he tore buildings down, he gutted them, he found ingenious ways of supporting their crumbling characterful old façades so that he could supply a multi-unit building behind it.

He enjoyed his immersion in work, and he stayed in his office through lunch – Rosalie served him a tuna fish sandwich on wholewheat toast – no salt, no mayonnaise, no butter; a layer of beansprouts; an apple for dessert.

Rosalie brought him a memo from Frank Keedy, one of his advance men. Keedy's brilliance lay in establishing paper trails among Chicago real estate brokers, and his memo spoke of his having uncovered a secret scheme for a building nearby – on Federal and Harrison – to be signed over to what Keedy was certain was a sweatshop:

a hundred Hispanics, Vietnamese or whoever, making dresses. Such a scheme made a developer like Parker seem almost idealistic. He looked out of his office window, and he was annoyed that he could not see the building from where he sat.

At the end of the day, he gave Rosalie the tapes he had filled with dictation: he had filled four loops.

'Got some typing for you.'

He saw her wince, and he knew what she was thinking: that there was two days' typing here, that he had cleaned his desk and dealt with all the files and memos, that he was amazing – the boss from hell.

'I was planning to come in late tomorrow, Mr Jagoda.' She kept her lips together so that nothing more would slip out. But she couldn't contain it. 'I've got an appointment at the hairdressers at nine-thirty.' She hunched her shoulders, afraid of what she would say.

'That's all right,' he said, smiling to reassure her. 'This can wait.'

He liked the gratitude in her eyes, he liked the way she relaxed. *He's so kind*, she was thinking. She would tell her friends that, he knew.

At six he met Barbara outside the Museum of Contemporary Art. The banners hanging from the façade were limp, in long folds, without a nudge of wind, and they seemed stiff – not like loose fabric, but like painted iron – without any movement at all in the early evening. This grey heat, and the shadows and the traffic fumes, seemed worse than it had at noon.

'I'm all sticky,' Barbara said, grazing Parker's cheek with her lips. 'Can you believe this heat?'

'I like it,' Parker said. 'What are you looking at?'

Barbara was staring at him looking thoroughly confused.

'You told me yesterday you hated it.'

'Maybe I meant the humidity.'

'No – you said –'

Parker seized her and held her until she laughed in a wild panicky way, protesting so loudly that she forgot what she had just said. And when he released her – she was flustered, angry, giddy – it was as though she had just come back to earth after a spell at a high altitude. They went into the Mapplethorpe exhibition.

Ronald Jakes, a fashion photographer, had insisted that Barbara see his friend's show. She was assembling a new portfolio, returning to modelling after almost two years away from it. Now that Eddie was six months old and could easily be looked after, and fed by a baby-sitter, Barbara felt easier about going back to work, she said. She had been exercising: she was a little heavier but she was firmer than she had been two years ago. She was eager to return to work – not for the money, but for the activity, being busy. So she said. Parker agreed with everything she said, as though he cared.

The people wandering into the exhibition were a fore-taste of the pictures – they were strangely dressed, ill-assorted, young men with bushy moustaches and shaven heads: not showing off, as people sometimes did at exhibitions, but trying to be anonymous, always looking away, and none of them talking above a murmur. That was the most ominous sign, the muttering silence hanging like twisting smoke among all those framed photographs.

'Oh, God,' Barbara said, with a low groan.

She was walking ahead of Parker, glancing sideways at the wall.

Parker squinted and kept walking. He did not want to stop and examine these pictures. They were of bald black men hugging bald white men, and they all had smooth buttocks and thick cocks. Some pictures were no more than cocks – like torpedoes, and some like cigars, and one like an over-ripe banana. It was naked men embracing, and naked men pointing, and naked men as silhouettes, and some hugging lamp-posts. There were photographs of flowers, too: big white blossoms with thick perfect petals, and large stark vegetables. Parker thought: The flowers have no odour, the vegetables have no taste. The rest was raw.

Barbara was walking slowly, uncertainly, wanting Parker to say something, he knew. The pictures were much stranger than she had anticipated, and where would she fit in here?

'What do you think?' she said.

'Apparently this Mapplethorpe is a homosexual,' Parker said loudly, making his expression as solemn as possible. He knew that the people near him heard, and were too frightened to say anything themselves. He despised them for shuffling past the pictures, and peering, and accepting it all.

Three panels showed a young man urinating in an arc into the mouth of a man kneeling before him.

'They've got beards, they're wearing hats, and look at their old coats,' Parker said, and stooped to find the title. ' "Dave and Gary. Sausalito." '

They passed another showing a man's whipped genitals, just that, wet and wounded, and it reminded Parker of a small animal that had been run over in the road: burst and bloody and flayed from the beating of heavy traffic, all those wheels. There was a man sewn into a skin-tight leather suit – he looked like a burned cat and had a German name, another title. There was a mock crucifixion, a white naked body lying on the floor of a dark forest, a penis like a pistol.

Parker said, 'Is that a zucchini or a pecker? It's hard to tell the difference. Here's another guy wearing a hat –

41

they love cowboy hats! The titles are terrific. "Kurt". "Jim". "North Sedgewick Street". Another Sausalito. I was in Sausalito last year, and I didn't see that bald bare-assed man crouched on that fire hydrant. That *is* a fire hydrant and not another pecker, isn't is?'

Barbara said, 'It's easy to make jokes about pictures that take so many risks.'

'Not as easy as you think, darling,' Parker said. 'I mean, sure these images are stark. They're totally re-ductive, and he's removed all context. So what you have is a kind of ikon, and it's not obscene, because it doesn't touch on any other reality.'

Barbara was squinting at him. He knew that squint. It meant she had listened long enough.

'It's crap,' Parker said. 'And the people at this exhibition are just as bad. They're the kind of people who put personal ads in the paper saying they're interested in leather, and water sports and could they please have an enema slave.'

'He does fashion photography, too. Just like Ronald Jakes. They're supposed to be really good.'

Parker said, 'You're actually interested in this guy!' He was annoyed that she didn't share his sense of outrage, that she hadn't understood any of his sarcasm, that she was even somewhat excited by the bald heads and swollen cocks – and was that weight-lifter a man or a woman?

'Helmut Newton gets weird like this, and he's great in fashion shots.'

But Parker was moving fast and still talking, 'These pictures say, "I know these people and you don't." "These people will do anything for me." "You couldn't meet these people if you tried – and yet I see them all the time." "These are my friends." "These are my lovers." It's all boasting.'

'You're angry,' Barbara said. 'You're never funny when you're angry.'

'It's sexual snobbery,' Parker said, his eye drawn to the hard black line that was the shadow of a clamp on a man's cock.

Barbara was smiling. She said, 'You're shocked.'

'If you're not there's something wrong with you,' Parker said.

'So you don't want to meet him?'

'I want to meet him very much.' And Parker went further, proposing that they take the photographer to dinner at N.E.W. Cuisine on West Erie, but when they called Jakes he insisted they meet at a newly decorated bar called 'Tracks' at Union Station. Like the florist and the news-stand on either side of it, it had the look of having tumbled away from the wall – there were tables on the concourse in front of the bar, just as there were flowers in racks on the left, and stacks of newspapers on the right. At a table near those papers – separated by a low fence to give this area the look of a French sidewalk café – the small man sat, hunched forward, smoking: Ronald Jakes.

A *National Enquirer* on a rack at the news-stand was headlined '*Cary Grant's Secrets – His Wild Temper, His Male Lovers, How He Dressed in Women's Underwear. Pictures Page 4.*'

'I'd rather sit inside,' Parker said.

He had a sense of people walking back and forth – pacing a few feet away; a sense of motion and intrusion, people flicking pages, browsing, killing time, glancing directly at him.

'It's all non-smoking inside,' Jakes said.

'Perfect,' Parker said, but he saw that Barbara had already seated herself – she did it elegantly, in a stately way, touching her knee with her fingertips as she eased that leg over the other and holding her head up and straightening her neck.

'We've just come from the Mapplethorpe exhibition.'

Jakes said nothing. He was small, pale, thin, he looked fragile and ill, he had blue irritable eyes. His hair was sparse – probably his smoking, Parker thought, smokers so often went bald and lame. The little man had a glass in his hand and was sitting sideways in a chair in a way that made Parker uncomfortable – he wanted to jerk him up straight. Still, he said nothing.

'It was incredible,' Barbara said.

'He's got the whole city down on him,' Jakes said. His voice quavered slightly in a way that was appropriate to his pale face and the large adam's apple jumping in his throat. The big name on the museum banner 'Mapplethorpe' was probably an insignificant little fussbudget in sneakers, like this man Jakes. 'You'd think they'd never seen a prick before.'

Parker said, 'Maybe they'd never seen one with a hose-clamp on it, or squashed and bleeding like it was hit by a Mack truck, or –'

'Parker, don't be silly,' Barbara said, and to Jakes she said, 'I think they're incredibly powerful.'

But Jakes's pale eyes were still on Parker.

'That's how life is,' he said. 'People look like that. People wear those clothes. People do those things.'

And the repeated word 'people' made each of them glance aside, beyond the edge of the bar, where people were hurrying to trains or loitering at the news-stand or choosing flowers. These people, Parker felt, disproved everything in Mapplethorpe's hideous pictures.

'How do I know they're not just posing for him – that he's paying them to perform?'

Jakes smiled at that, and Parker sensed that the little man needed disapproval much more than he needed encouragement.

'You want to pretend they don't exist,' Jakes said. 'But

they do – and more than that. There's a lot of beauty in those bodies. You lead a very sheltered life, my friend.'

'Maybe I do,' Parker said, and saying it he felt defiant and pure. He liked the thought, and he believed it to be true, and he saw himself as rather naive and shockable, with a strong sense of the absurd because of it – you had to be shockable in order to make jokes.

'I thought we were going to talk about my portfolio,' Barbara said.

'If we're talking about Mapplethorpe then we're talking about your portfolio, sweetheart,' Jakes said, addressing Barbara but keeping his eyes on Parker.

There was a density to the man's concentration that made Parker self-conscious. And the people at the newsstand didn't help – they were glancing into the bar, looking up from their newspapers. Parker kept having the sense of a crowd gathering, and it dispersed whenever he looked over. The people distracted him – what had Jakes just said? – and even when he turned his back on them he saw their hot faces and staring eyes in the mirror.

'Something wrong?' Jakes said. Parker felt the man was being clumsily affectionate. 'Want a real drink?'

'I don't drink alcohol.'

'That makes two of us,' Jakes said. 'Have one of these. It's just bloody mary mix.'

'Acid, guar gum, stabilizers,' Parker said, with his mouth turned down. 'Salt.'

Jakes turned to Barbara and pursed his lips and shuddered, hugging himself with his bony arms.

'And maybe you have to lead a sheltered life to understand and pity those poor exploited people in Mapplethorpe's pictures,' Parker said. 'Because he's using them and they don't know it.'

'Maybe they want to be used,' Jakes said, and smiled

for the first time, turning as he did so, and in that circuit taking in the people carrying bags and briefcases, the hot rumpled late-going commuters, the people at the newsstand. 'I can tell you that some of them want to be abused.'

'Then they're dumb and pitiful,' Parker said. 'And that's the worst kind of exploitation – they don't know any better.'

Jakes whistled and rolled his eyes and he said to Barbara, 'Where did you get her, sweetie?'

'I look at those pictures and I see victims,' Parker said.

'My pictures are about pleasure,' Jakes said. 'Ditto Mapplethorpe. In his best self-portrait he has a bullwhip rammed up his ass.'

Someone on the other side of the fence was muttering loudly; Parker couldn't make out the words, but the sound was vicious. Parker said, 'Couldn't we find a quieter place?'

'Gays used to have all the secrets,' Jakes said in a nagging way. 'But they don't any more. I think the so-called straights have a problem. They're the ones with all the secrets now. Listen, married people would never let Mapplethorpe photograph them like those gays did.'

'I wonder why,' Parker said.

'You don't want me to take pictures of your wife,' Jakes said. 'So you're inventing an objection to Robert's exhibition.'

'That's not true,' Barbara said, and in her sudden anger she sat forward and lost her beauty.

'How do you know?'

'Because he would have told me,' Barbara said. 'We tell each other everything. We have no secrets.'

The photographer said, 'You know where to find me, but you won't be back,' and glanced away as Parker took Barbara's hand and led her away – out of the bar, past the

46

news-stand. When she hesitated near the stack of evening papers, Parker tightened his grip on her and steered her forward.

'I worry about you,' he said.

'Darling,' she said, with love and gratitude, and she let him lead her through the station into the hot evening.

'I'm hungry,' Barbara said.

They found a restaurant on Monroe, a dark place with heavy chairs and the door propped open, the business lunch still featured on the blackboard and men in shirtsleeves at the bar.

A waitress in a frilly blouse brought menus, but Parker waved the menu away.

'No oil, no salt, no MSG, no colouring, no flavouring, no sugar, no white flour, no butter,' he said. 'What do you have?'

He was brought a dry spinach salad with chickpeas, and a baked potato which he burst and filled with yogurt. He drank seltzer. For dessert he had a bowl of mixed berries.

Barbara had prime rib and fries.

'Dead animals,' Parker said. 'Greasy blood.'

It was their joke, but Parker was frowning and snatching at his face. He put his fingers to his lips and began to pluck wildly, whimpering as he did so. And finally after some effort he drew his fingers slowly from his tongue and looked down in horror.

'I had a hair in my mouth!'

Later, driving back home, the thought of it made him nauseous and he pulled into the breakdown lane on Lake Shore Drive and violently vomited.

4

HE was anxious about Ewa at midnight, but by dawn his anxiety had dwindled to no more than curiosity, and he got out of bed wondering whether to call her from his home phone. But what was the point? She was all right. He imagined her waiting for his call, but this waiting in itself – his not calling her – kept her safe indoors: he saw a great placid shape of a shadowy woman sitting by a telephone.

'More forest fires,' Parker said, and the picture shattered on the screen as he dug his thumb into the remote button.

He was talking to himself; Barbara was downstairs with the baby, dressing him for the trip to her mother's, and calling out for Parker to turn the air-conditioning up – it was going to be another day in the nineties.

He remembered how on these hot days Ewa spoke of taking showers – sometimes four in an afternoon to keep cool. Her mention of these showers and the window ('Never any breeze,' she said) helped him visualize her apartment, the small rooms, the still air, the smells. She spoke of music bothering her neighbours, the way she lay in bed listening to her Walkman with the buttons in her ears. It was one of those places on the south side where you always heard voices and pipes and stifled shouts. Yet she never complained. If she had he would have known something about her.

'I'm taking the Beemer,' he said, and began to hurry, because the suspicion was growing in him that he might be wrong, that Ewa might be in trouble.

That thought so possessed him that he took one of the Morton Grove exits on the Edens Expressway and found a phone in a laundromat.

'*This is urgent,*' he said slowly to Ewa's answering machine. Where could she possibly be at eight-ten in the morning? He had no idea where she worked, or whether she worked at all. All he knew about her was contained in the letter she had sent in reply to his personal ad – that, and the fact that she was beautiful and didn't seem to know it.

Leaving the message for her to call him, he became passionate and anxious, looking around at the frothing windows of the washing machines in the launderama, the dirty houses, the blistered paint and scorched cars.

Then, moving on, down the Kennedy under a steamy sky, he regretted what he said – not because it had been rash but because it was probably too late to help her.

At the parking garage on Wells, Vern – so the badge sewn on his shirt pocket said – handed him a ticket and seemed glad to see him.

'Hey, we missed you,' Vern said. 'You've been taking the train, or what is it, maybe parking somewhere else?'

'I've been out of town,' Parker said.

'Business or pleasure?'

The man was slow and obstructive, and had a dim-witted smile. He hung on to the window with both hands, leaning towards Parker. He had coffee on his breath and sugar grains on his lips from the doughnut he had eaten.

Parker said, 'Do you know anyone who goes to Detroit for pleasure?'

'Some fine places in Detroit, if you know where to find them. Hey, what was the weather like?'

Parker said, 'Just like this.'

'I heard they've been having rain,' Vern said.

Parker had the uncomfortable feeling that this man might be teasing him, and he had always hated teasing for being the cruellest method of entrapment.

'A little rain is worse than none,' Parker said, trying to ease the car forward.

'They let you water your grass up in Evanston?'

'I don't live in Evanston any more,' Parker said. 'I'm in Morton Grove now – the Skokie end. You know the place that makes limited edition plates near the launder-ama off exit eighteen? Around there.'

'Yeah?' Vern said, and looked concerned. 'How come you sold?'

'I had to,' Parker said, and felt the man needed to be told a calamity – Vern still had a hungry querying look on his face. 'We had some unforeseen medical bills. I had to raise some cash in a hurry –'

Vern still looked unsatisfied, and he was holding tight to the car and still breathing hard. He winced to show his sympathy for Parker and yet he wanted more. The man's reaction provoked Parker, who felt he had become the man he had just described – in Morton Grove with medical bills – and had a right to be left alone.

'I'm late for a dentist's appointment,' he said.

'Sorry,' Vern said. 'There's spaces on Level Five.'

He drove up the ramp. He sorrowed for himself. He was that hard-pressed man who had moved to a smaller house in a bad neighbourhood for financial reasons: the result of a serious operation.

And it was almost possible, he reasoned. Barbara had had to wear a neck-brace for most of April, and an operation would have cost him, even with his medical coverage. He should have said to Vern, *I didn't realize that I was in a very vulnerable position*. He convinced himself, too, that he could very easily have spent the past two days in Detroit.

He parked on Level Seven in a corner behind a pillar and sat in the car several minutes before getting out and looking for the fire stairs. At the back exit he laughed, noticing the yellow and black symbol that meant this dark and hard-to-get-at place had been designated an approved shelter for a radioactive emergency.

The telephone rang soon after Parker unlocked his desk. It was a woman, talking fast, and for a moment Parker could not place her, didn't know her, found her voice an intrusion, was it a wrong number? He was thinking of that blue peeling house across from the launderama, the shabby porch, the hot black shingles on the roof, the junked burned-out car in the street. The house seemed very sad and important to him.

'You all right? You sounded really wired,' the woman said.

Ewa. He remembered everything in that instant: the alarm he had felt, his fears for her safety, the phone in the stinging soapy air of the launderama.

'I'm fine,' Parker said. He saw Ewa plainly now, and he had the strongest urge to be with her, to protect her. But instead of worrying her by saying *You are in great danger* – the words were clearly framed in his mind – he said, 'I have to see you as soon as possible.'

'Tonight, yeah. We've got a date. That's the arrangement.'

'Never mind the arrangement,' Parker said. 'This is urgent. Listen –'

'What is it?' she said, so innocently, so pleadingly, that he heard in her plaintive voice a lonely person who was doomed – marked out for it, as though she was already under the staring eye of a violent and pitiless man who planned to trap her.

'Do you know the big parking garage on North Wells in the Loop? My car is on Level Seven – a blue Beemer. Meet me there at noon.'

Ewa said nothing, and when he prodded her, she hesitated.

'I'm not going to hurt you,' he said.

'I know,' she said awkwardly, as though she knew she was being unreasonable. 'But I don't knock off here until half-past one – I mean, I'm at work now.'

'Where's work?' Parker said.

'Flipping Whoppers,' Ewa said.

'You think I'm joking.'

'I just called home,' Ewa said. 'I got your message off my machine. You sounded pretty worried.'

'Maybe you're the one who should be worried,' Parker said. 'Okay. Meet me at the garage at two. Level Seven.'

He was calm when he put the phone down. He knew there were people who needed secretaries and assistants and listeners – who were strengthened and made to feel they mattered, because these others were nearby. Not him: he never felt stronger or more imaginative or resourceful than when he was by himself. When he was alone he was a giant, and he pitied those people who suffered because they were solitary – people who secretly felt they were going nuts, because they had no one to talk to, and so many of them were women watching their lives narrowing, the years just drying up and leaving a residue of dust.

In this mood of authority and pity he roughed out a possible use for the building on South Federal. It was just behind Printers' Square, which had already been renovated, and which contained enough people to make a multi-use complex in its original brick shell commercially viable. The thing was to get it zoned commercial as well as residential, and then use the upper storeys with their views for condo units – and there might be roof-space to hide another storey; down below there would be plenty of room for boutiques, restaurants and stores selling select stuff like designer food.

Rosalie came late, and explained once again about the hairdresser.

'Like it? It cost me eighty-five bucks.'

Loosely frizzed and coloured hair, so ugly and conspicuous, she looked as though she had been electrocuted by the fag who'd overcharged her, and why? Because a few days ago she had probably sat in her apartment feeling miserable and thinking *I'll get my hair done and feel better*.

'I'm going to take action on Keedy's memo about that sweatshop scheme on South Federal,' Parker said, around one o'clock. 'It might be just what I've been looking for.'

Rosalie smiled but so vacuously that Parker knew that she didn't have the slightest idea of what he was talking about.

'The site,' he said, knowing that he sounded like a perfectionist, and rather proud ot it. 'I'll be dealing with it this afternoon if anyone calls.'

He left the office, fully intending to pass the sweatshop later in the day – the memory had roused him, the image of the overworked and exploited woman he envisioned touched him, and he walked into the hot street feeling peculiarly strong, as he always did when he had just said something that he knew to be true. Gutting that building would liberate them.

He was glad to have the rumour of this sweatshop. It was not simply that he was running out of possible sites in the downtown area. It had something to do with ridding the building of a shady operation and saving those women who were at risk. It was rescue; it was renovation; it was money.

Ewa Womack was also at risk. He made his way down under the black shadow of the El that split the light beneath it. There was a bitter smell of rusting iron in the air here, at this margin of the Loop. He sniffed it and he was conscious of his moving slowly and deliberately, as though he were being watched. But it was he who was doing the watching: he felt important but invisible to other people. He was excitedly aware of himself knifing silently through the shadows and the steaming crowd.

He did not go into the garage by the Wells Street entrance. He told himself that he was in a hurry and slipped into the alley behind it on LaSalle, that he had found one day by accident, blunderingly looking for an exit. It was just the sort of entryway that made a garage like this a perfect place for muggers.

Running up to Level Seven did not leave him breathless – for that energy he credited his diet – the banana, the bran muffin and carob yogurt he'd had mid-morning, for example; but the tramping of his feet on the stairs and that swift sound on the landing seemed to alarm Ewa, who stepped out from beside the car and faced him, knees bent, looking fierce, and he clattered to a halt.

'I'm not even winded,' he said. 'Want to know why?'

She was too startled to say anything – but he was smiling. He looked around. There were only two other cars, there were no other people, and the narrow glaring windows at the back of the building only blackened the shadows on this level, that was like a deep shelf.

'Why did we have to meet here?' Ewa said, and he could hear a tremor in her voice.

'It just seemed simpler.'

That was almost enough to calm her – he was walking past her to unlock her door. Her fear was like an odour. He gave her plenty of room, he didn't touch her, he didn't look into her eyes at all.

'I didn't know you had a car like this,' she said.

'People see a Beemer and they don't even notice that it's six years old,' Parker said.

'Right, because this one is two years old.'

'What are you, a dealer?' he said. He was impressed, because women were blind when it came to cars, and even when you told them they didn't remember the year or the model. They just wanted it to look sharp and to start on the first twist of the key.

Ewa said, 'People steal these.'

'Which people?'

'Punks. Crack-heads.'

'How do you know that?'

'I'm not stupid,' Ewa said. 'I've got eyes.'

Parker let her in and then went around to his side and got in behind the wheel. He inserted the key into the ignition, but he didn't turn it. He sat sideways and looked at Ewa, his eyes on hers for the first time.

'You should open your eyes,' he said. 'You don't know what could happen to you.'

Ewa turned to him, reacting slowly, as though translating, and again her fear seemed to penetrate the air like a sharp smell.

'A woman like you could get hurt,' Parker said.

Ewa made no apparent motion and yet Parker sensed that she moved – within her clothes, within her body, a tightening of the strings of her muscles, hardening her flesh.

'I thought we were going somewhere,' she said.

And her eyes: she was darting them left and right, and looking at her reflection in the side window, in the mirror. Her whole body was coiling and contracting. And she was mostly in shadow, so this was not light and motion but rather a subtle chafing of the darkness and no more than a slight whisper of her anxious legs crossing.

'Not yet, darling,' he said.

The affectionate word was like the threatening glitter of a blade and had that same effect on her. He heard a small catch in her breathing.

'I have things to do this afternoon,' she said.

Before she folded her arms and sat more compactly in the seat she glanced out of the back window at the oily floor of Level Seven, and the ramp to Six – and Parker looked too. It was so quiet and dark it was as though they were underground: nothing there but the dark.

'That can wait' – he did not say *darling*, she was already fearful enough – 'I need to talk to you.'

She said, 'You're talking to me like you know me,' and she smiled to show him that she thought this was absurd.

'I know you better than you think.'

That seemed to put her on guard and she unfolded her arms and let her fingers graze the door-latch and snag it; but the door didn't open, there was no sound and there should have been a click.

'Central locking,' Parker said, into her face.

'I was looking for the window button,' she said in a whisper. 'I need some air.'

She was lying about the window button, he knew. She had been trying the door. But it was also true that the afternoon heat had thickened around them and the darkness on Level Seven was as hot as a blanket and seemed to lay over them in a woolly and suffocating way.

Then her whisper seemed like an effect of that same heat.

'Because I'm a woman? And you think you know women? That is such bullshit.'

Parker had begun to perspire and was enjoying the sensation of sweat moving down his face, and his wet shirt tightened and restrained him as it was plastered against him.

'We've had ten drinks, the whole time I've known you.' She was challenging him but softly, as though encouraging him to be reasonable. He could see she was very afraid.

Parker saw that the shadowy curve on her cheek was like the curve on her thigh.

'Let's get out of here,' she said.

'To your place?' There was a gumminess on his tongue as he spoke.

'Never mind that.'

It was like a rebuke and yet he felt energized by it, as though he had revealed that she was capable of being calm.

'So what's the story?' she said.

And then he remembered. He waited a moment, until she fidgeted again, and finally he spoke in a low voice which itself was full of whispers.

'When I was at Northwestern I was in a fraternity,' he said. 'Every Saturday night one of the brothers used to bring a girl to his room, and every single time he scored – the girl would leave with the pale dazed look of someone who's been screwed ragged. This guy never struck out. What was his secret?'

Parker paused to make sure that Ewa was listening and then he resumed.

'We hid a mike under his bed. We left it on and tape-recorded everything that went on from the moment he shut the door until the moment he left. After they were gone, we listened to the tape – and we were shocked. We heard him and the girl in the room, and the first thing he did was threaten her and tell her to strip – "Or I'll cut your face so bad –"'

He was still staring hard at the black shadows cutting across Ewa's face.

'You heard her gasp, and then he was on her. She

didn't have time to scream. She was whimpering – we heard that. And we heard the bed, the silly sinister bed-springs going oink-oink-oink. Then more silence, her whimpering and gagging, and we guessed what was happening then, too.'

He stopped, but Ewa said nothing.

'He tied her up,' Parker said. 'Very tight.'

He moved closer to her and put his arms around her in a consoling way, and his other hand lay in her lap until her legs shut like scissors and she recoiled, hardening again and becoming stronger.

'That's the kind of guy I'm talking about,' Parker said.

Ewa exhaled slowly and seemed to swell and strengthen as she did so. 'That's rape,' she said. 'That's aggravated assault. I'd kill the bastard. I hate that story.'

Parker let go. The shadows had not left her cheeks, nor had she moved; but his soaked shirt had gone cold against his back and he felt his skin shrinking on his face.

'I think you're going to be all right,' he said, and he had a sense of relief, as though he too had been saved. 'So let's go. How about a smile?'

Her face was lovely and sculpted, and lovelier still for its unsmiling melancholy. She simply looked at him and put her tongue against her lips, though when he started the car she relaxed again.

'I could use a coffee,' she said.

'There's manganese in coffee,' he said. 'Supposed to be very good for you.'

5

HE wondered *Has something changed?* because he had felt so much better in these past few days. He woke feeling refreshed and almost virtuous, as though he had risen purified from a deep watery well. The well was sleep. It was a kind of death. He did not dream – or if he did he could remember nothing. That was unusual. He had always liked sleep from the dreams it gave him.

He was simpler now, he knew that. He felt free of any sexual desire. The urge had, it seemed, been torn out of him – uprooted like a carrot, and there was now crisp daylight where there had been thick wavering shadow. The light was the reason he was now able to see so clearly. Ewa, the other day – he hadn't even touched her except to comfort her. It was a good feeling: no blood throbbing in his eyes, the triumph of admiring a woman and not wanting to possess her.

'You've got a date tomorrow,' Barbara said in a reminding way, as he was dressing. She still lay in bed, and she looked like part of the bed, her loose hair, her nightgown twisted at her breasts.

He knew what she meant, but something in the word disturbed him, and he said nothing – didn't want to think of it. When she switched on the television, he continued to dress. He didn't hear it, didn't see it, and later at breakfast (oat-bran porridge, Postum, a tangerine, dry wholemeal toast) he paid no attention to the yakking radio.

He drove himself to the station, avoiding the news-stand at the station.

To anyone who commented on the fact that he didn't have his usual *Tribune* in his hand he planned to say forcefully: I haven't looked at a newspaper for ages. I don't read the goddamned things any more. They're all run by Republicans and its the same stuff every day. Most of it is lies, and you end up with ink on your fingers. If there's something happening everyone knows about it – it's in the air.

The presidential campaign was happening, and that was the best reason of all not to buy a paper. What a choice, and you knew they were awful when you saw their wives – four bossy bitches propping up their greedy eager-to-please husbands.

'They make me feel violent, too,' he would have added, meaning the newspapers.

He looked for a good seat. He hated people whispering on the train, and people who looked hard at him and then turned away and muttered – he saw some of those sneaks. He saw an empty seat next to a stout neatly-dressed man who held a large briefcase on his lap – no newspaper. Parker commented on that: 'We're the only two people on this train that don't have their noses in a paper.'

'I get mine at the office,' the man said. 'I don't even have time to read it.'

Then Parker made his speech against newspapers, and the man smiled and became friendly. He said he was involved in asbestos and chemical disposal.

Parker said, 'That's a terribly risky business. I'm well acquainted with the problems.'

'Aw, I'm just a glorified junk dealer,' the man said.

'No, no,' Parker said. 'Listen, I'm a high school principal and all our pipes were once insulated in asbestos. We had to close the school and clear out every bit of it. Masks. Gloves. Suits. The whole nine yards. It was very complex.'

'Most people don't understand that,' the man said, and looked pleased.

'So I know where you're coming from,' Parker said.

There was pride in the man's smile as he said, 'It's a messy business. You wouldn't believe the insurance I have to pay for my guys. People think it's easy. But as you say, it's a high-risk, high-gain business.'

Parker thought with satisfaction how he had not said that at all.

'And you're rendering a public service,' Parker said.

'I guess I do all right,' the man said, gently pleased with himself. He had narrow shoulders and a big belly and a Masonic ring, and Parker reflected on the accuracy of what the man had said, how he *did* look like a glorified junk dealer. He was still smiling. 'Where's your school?'

What school? Parker thought, and then remembered.

'Lincoln High School, over on Sedgwick, near Superior. It's a large granite building with a clock on the front that shows the wrong time. We've got almost two thousand students.'

There was no such school. Parker faced the man and silently challenged him to deny any of it.

'I've heard of it,' the man said, and when Parker said nothing, the man added, 'I've heard good things about it.'

He accepted it, accepted the students, the principal, invented the good reputation, bought it all, because like most people – Parker knew this – he was just thinking of himself and did nothing but move his mouth.

'You still got a problem with your insulation?'

That was typical. Parker had been talking about his school and all the man had heard was the mention of the asbestos.

'We've got an old bomb shelter we haven't looked at.'

The man plucked a business card from his wallet. It was grandly lettered *Baskies Waste Intervention*. Parker fingered the card and then began to pity the man.

'That's me: Harry Baskies. My accountant thought up the name – not bad, eh?'

He was still thinking of himself – you could see it in his fleshy face – as he turned to smile at the window. Parker imagined the man looking at his face in the bedroom mirror, and shaving it, scraping slowly at his cheeks and around his lips – and it seemed to him almost tragic that he performed this futile task on the same face every day.

Parker was going to speak again, but he stopped himself when he saw that they were at Clark and Division. He could see the Marlboro sign. The man heaved himself out of his seat.

He was sorry there wasn't time to say more. He felt expansive, inventive, energetic. He could convince people that he had just piloted a supertanker down the Saint Lawrence Seaway. That he had recently returned from an extended trip in Europe. That he had been severely injured in a cycling accident. That he'd had a quarter of a million dollars wiped off the value of his shares in the Stock Market crash on Black Monday. That he was a wholesaler of swimming pool chemicals and appliances. And he wanted afterwards to look closely at the faces of his listeners.

More than anything he wanted to meet an intelligent woman. She would appreciate his telling her the secret he had discovered – and this was a fact. That we are all, all human beings, travelling down parallel lines from birth to death. The parallel lines were the reason each person was so lonely – everyone Parker had ever met. But not Parker himself.

Parker had managed to cut across, to converge: he did not travel in a straight line. Was it a sign he saw, or the fact that the train was drawing into LaSalle, that made him think of the word *Loop*? Whatever, it was the right word. His whole life was a curve and in the course of his life he would inscribe a loop. He had escaped the tyranny of parallel lines.

So far the loop was incomplete, and yet what amazing things he'd seen, what people he'd met, what secrets he knew.

Many different people needed him, because he knew how to reassure them, like the junk dealer on the train, who had gone away very pleased with himself. Ewa needed him, too. He did not know where she lived or where she worked. There was so much to discover in her – he had so many ways of finding out. And yesterday he had been thrilled by the conversation in the locked car, in the parking garage. And he thought how she might be that intelligent woman he could divulge his secrets to: she would understand.

At the office, Rosalie said, 'How about your date yesterday?'

He hated her for making him remember Ewa, for confusing him, for saying that word, for reminding him of what Barbara had said, *You've got a date tomorrow.* Dating always suggested to him the steady routine of sex and smiles, like people blindly eating, lifting their hands to their mouths, stuffing themselves with predictable and joyless motions.

He almost shouted, his face darkened, but she meant the place at Harrison and South Federal.

'You don't acquire valuable sites by knocking on the

door and asking people if they're violating labour laws,' Parker said.

Rosalie became very quiet and round-shouldered, and her new hairstyle – that wig of teased and twisted strands – made her look pathetic, as though someone had clapped it on her head to make a fool of her.

'Is there another way, Parker?'

It was Frank Keedy, looking hot – his shirt damp and discoloured, his face flushed – as he entered Parker's office.

'You scope it out. You use a little cunning,' Parker said. 'You don't knock. You don't send out signals.'

'But you keep appointments maybe,' Keedy said. 'I told you on the memo that Kegler Textiles was at the end of that paper trail, and that they had already agreed a closing for the building. If we don't move fast on that property it's going to be scooped by some Arab and run into the ground so that he can use it for depreciation.'

'You think I want to lose money on it?' Parker said.

'No, but you're not going to turn it into a toilet,' Keedy said. 'Or if you do, it'll be a pay toilet.'

'Know what heat-stroke is?' Parker said.

Keedy compressed his lips and sighed raspily through his nose, but he had already started to back away.

'Any idea of the devastating effect it has on a six-month old baby – chills, convulsions, a temperature of a hundred and four?'

Keedy began apologizing in a drawl.

Parker cut him off by saying, 'That's what I was dealing with yesterday.'

And when Keedy had retreated the whole way to the door and apologized again, Parker turned his back on him and zipped his briefcase and said, 'I was just going to South Federal.'

'I staked it out already,' Keedy said, and Parker could

tell from his tone – it was almost sorrowful – that the man was abject. 'There's eighty-seven people going in there at six in the morning, and there's light still burning at night. They're all women. They're mostly Hispanics. There might be a language barrier. You could take Perez.'

'I'm looking for a site,' Parker said. 'It's not a social call.'

'The last guy I worked for, LeBaron, never left the office,' Keedy said. 'Had no idea how to renovate property. He was just an advertising man.'

Keedy was clumsily trying to compliment him, and yet Parker had the feeling that this other man – his predecessor – was good and conscientious, a simple fellow who ate badly and had no secrets.

It was a big brown building behind Printers' Row, and Parker was sure that it would be no problem to scoop out its brick shell. It was probably being rented cheaply by someone who would move as soon as a sale was final, that it was semi-derelict and looked unused and was probably a fire-trap. It was so dilapidated it had never been under suspicion. Anyone would walk past without stopping: the IRS, the city, Immigration, the cops. Only the toughest developer would be attracted, and there were fewer of those around these days with interest rates so high. Still, Parker knew he had competition.

He lurked for a while, looking up. The eleventh and twelfth floors were definitely occupied – most of the windows tilted open because of the heat, some of them painted or stuck over and blocked with paper. He hesitated, he tried the door – locked. He walked around to the front and saw that the main door was boarded up. So here was a building that was regarded as empty – never mind the IRS and Immigration, this was a violation of the city fire ordinances. People working in a building with a boarded-up door! No exit! He went to the rear once again, and this time he saw someone move inside.

'Hello,' he said. 'Open up.'

The woman opened her mouth, and behind the glass looked like a fish gargling in a tank. Perhaps she was speaking? Parker couldn't hear. He made a motion with his hand that meant he didn't understand, and another gesture for her to open up. The woman looked worried. Parker smiled and shrugged, and made himself appear harmless. Then the woman seemed merely hesitant and flustered and fishlike again.

She cracked the door open. She said, *'No Inglés.'*

Parker shoved the door into her face, pushing the woman against the wall.

'That was your own fault,' he said on the stairs. He climbed one flight – listened; climbed another – listened. The woman down below was silent, probably terrified, but from above he heard the buzz of machines – the sound in the stairwell. He kept climbing four or five more flights, moving easily – a person on the average American sugary-salty-fatty diet would have given up on the ground floor or bitched until the elevator came, he knew that.

Someone above him was walking downstairs. He stopped. He heard a door open and shut; still listened – water running: it had to be the women's john. He crept towards the door and positioned himself there until the woman emerged: dark hair, dark eyes, an Indian face. She stared straight ahead and walked past him without speaking, definitely *no Inglés*.

He waited, wondering whether to go on. Finally he mounted the stairs, but slowly – not wanting to come face to face with a room full of people or one of the goons that sometimes guarded these places. He needed to see them closely, though, and find a vantage point to shoot a picture on macro – an isolated pathetic face or a woman toiling at a machine; it would help, he thought, if she was attractive in an emaciated way, sort of beaten and beautiful.

A door slammed and feet began tip-tapping on the stairs, someone moving fast – a woman.

'Hello,' he said.

'Hi.' She was young, rather fat and pale, with heat blotches on her cheeks. She wore a tee-shirt and shorts and rubber flip-flops.

'Can I ask you a question?' Parker said. 'I'm from the fire department.'

'Give me a minute.'

She hurried through the door, into the toilet, and Parker walked away – did not want to hear anything, hated the very sound it made, the uncertain dribble of a woman on a hopper. She was soon on the landing, wiping her wet hands on her tee-shirt.

'Hey, did you smell smoke?'

She had thought that up while she'd been inside.

'That's good,' Parker said. 'I like it. No, we're just checking empty buildings in the area. Anyone upstairs?'

'Only about a billion people,' she said. 'What's wrong?'

Parker had begun to stare at her, and he had screwed up one eye.

'Nothing,' he said.

'Can't you hear the machines? All that racket? It's boiling hot and there's about two million Hispanics, all knitting and cutting and sewing like crazy.'

'How many exactly?'

'Who wants to know?'

'I told you,' Parker said. His body had gone sad and heavy for a reason he could not name, and the wonder-

67

ment in his head was also a kind of heaviness. He had to wet his lips and say, 'Fire department.'

'Because the union's been on our case, that's why I ask. They sent about five hundred –'

'Please,' Parker said. 'Just tell me –'

'Hey, mister,' she said, and smiled crookedly to show him she was being sarcastic.

'Are they all Hispanics?' Parker managed to say.

'Yeah. And the owner's from Iran. Don't believe any crap about Kegler Textiles being anything but Arab. Sadeek weighs about a ton, and he puts two gallons of grease on his hair and he's always hitting on us – I mean, me and my friend Sharon. We're the only white people here. I'm always saying "Sharon, there's got to be a better –"'

Parker could not listen. He became sadder. His tongue was too thick to allow him to speak. He took hold of the handrail and wondered if he was going to cry. It was possible. He did not want anyone to witness it – but this girl was a stranger, so it might not matter. Still, he had to leave. And he found it hard and dangerous to go down these steep flights of stairs.

'Hey, mister,' the girl was saying, as he descended. 'Hey, mister,' she said. 'Hey –'

Then it was tomorrow, and he felt it was crucial that he should keep his date.

At the hotel he knew exactly what the desk clerk was thinking: *If you live in Evanston and you're checking into this hotel in the Loop something must be wrong in your life.* Because the Blackstone was a fairly sleazy place, and all the more sleazy for trying to look respectable. It was always so dusty in the Loop, and June was a suffocating month.

But Parker just smiled at him – his way of refuting the

desk clerk's assumptions. His smile said, *Everything is fine in my life*.

'Will this be for one person or two?' the clerk asked with an obliqueness that was intended to be polite. He was still writing on Parker's registration card.

'Two.'

The clerk raised his eyes to Parker.

'Someone's joining me later.'

Someone was an alarmingly vague word – so was *joining*, so was *later*. There wasn't quite enough information in these words, but they were loaded with possible implications. Was someone a man? A woman? A child? Did joining mean staying, or sleeping, or what? And later might mean any time. Parker enjoyed the forced trying-to-be-businesslike look on the clerk's face. He liked speaking clearly to strangers and giving them no information.

In his room he looked everywhere to make sure it was clean: opened drawers, searched the closets, turned the bed down, examined the bathroom. He piled the pillows against the headboard and lay there, propped up, drinking the seltzer he had brought in his small bag, watching television. He decided on a wildlife documentary, having flicked through the news, the soaps, the Spanish channel, the cartoons, the weather. He sipped his seltzer and listened for the door and watched 'National Geographic Explorer', the eccentric nesting habits of the African widowbird. When his mind drifted back to yesterday's encounter at the sweatshop, he concentrated on the details of the movie, the vast mass of twigs, high on the thorn tree, that was the widowbird's nest, and on the long beautiful tail of the bird, which hung down and swayed as it flew.

The knock came at eight, and Parker switched off the television as he went to the door.

She was taller than he expected, and wearing a black

dress and red shoes. In spite of the heat she wore a silk scarf around her neck and tight buttoned gloves.

'Come on in,' he said, and she moved past him – all odour, perfume, hairspray, deodorant, even the smell of the Chicago streets, dust and exhaust and cigar smoke clung to her clothes, and it was like the world entering this little room.

She was still walking, not looking back at him, and now he saw she wore a small hat pinned to her hair.

'What's your name?'

'Vivian.'

'Isn't that one of those names that means something?'

She said, 'It means my mother used to go to the movies.'

She was uninterested in the room, she had been in so many just like this. Her attention was on Parker, and she seemed impatient to begin.

'Have a seat,' he said.

'That's okay,' she said. There was an edge to her voice, a slight note of irritation. But he was happy for her to stand and strut on those steep heels.

'You want to discuss money?'

She did not hesitate: her answer came as though she had prepared it.

'If it's a question of discussion I'm out of here right now.'

He faced her and nodded, conceding everything.

'Three hundred,' she said.

'What do I get for that?'

He had already started counting the money into her hand, and he was fascinated by her glove.

'A slave,' she said, and put the bills into her handbag and snapped its jaws shut.

She had said *slave* in a drawl and showed her teeth, and the word still trembled in the air as he watched her, admiring the fit of her dress, her lip gloss, her full breasts. There was a glow of perspiration on her face and neck. The shoes gave her height – she was nearly as tall as he was – and her perfume, mingled with the street smells, was like fragrant poison.

'You might be sorry you said that.'

'Make me sorry,' she said.

All along the outside wall of the hotel the air-conditioners seemed to scour the night with their whining motors. Hearing them, Parker could not understand why his hands were so damp. He sat down and became quiet, thinking hard; but no word came to him.

He said, 'Take your clothes off slowly, but leave your shoes on. Don't sit down. Don't take off any of your jewellery. I like that necklace, those bracelets, the earrings.'

She plucked off her gloves and then slipped out of her dress. Her long brown hair had highlights: red and gold in it, and it shook as she leaned and fumbled behind her back to loosen her bra. She flung the bra aside and used both hands to slide her panties down, and when they were at her ankles she stepped out of them. And then she stood naked before him, in her high heels, her jewellery catching the light from the lamp near the mirror.

'What do you want?' she said.

His lips were dry, and he shuddered slightly.

'I'm not moving,' he said – and he was glad she was not next to him, that she could not feel the tremor in him. 'I'm sitting here. Make love to yourself, and take your time.'

She seemed unsure of herself, and only now did she look around the room – awkwardly, until she glanced at her reflection in the mirror and then she clasped her breasts and sighed. She stroked herself between her legs, and moved her legs apart, and arched her back. Her hands moved caressingly over her body, her fingertips

71

active. Parker was aroused, seeing how she concentrated on herself in the mirror – how she ignored him. He was not there for her: that gave him pleasure, to see her own fingers against her skin. At first she seemed to prolong it, as though performing, but she quickened her movements, as though caught up in it and acting involuntarily. There was a catch in her throat and tension in her arms and legs. She gave out a great gasp of pleasure and then sank to her knees and hung her head. She was done.

After she got her breath – still kneeling – she came forward on all fours, towards him. Seeing her all his desire died, and when she touched him he felt only fear.

'Let me try,' she said. 'I know how.'

He stood up clumsily objecting and looked down at her, crouched beneath him.

'What is it?'

'Nothing,' he said, and sounded terrified. 'I'm not in the mood.' She reached for him again. He said, 'Please!' and it was a shriek.

Then the woman stood up and looked at him with enormous sympathy. She put her arms around him, and clasped her hands behind his back and hugged him. She was gentle; her body was warm against him.

'Don't think about it,' she said.

She took off her wig and wrapped herself in a towel.

'I'm going to call the baby-sitter,' she said, and dialled the number, sitting on the edge of the bed.

Parker felt small and dark in the big soft chair.

'It's Barbara,' he heard. 'Everything okay?'

Parker heard an unusual sound and was disgusted when he saw that it was Barbara scratching her head with the tip of her room key.

'Make sure he has enough to drink – it's so damned hot.' She turned to Parker, but still spoke into the phone. 'We won't be late – one at the latest.'

'Twelve,' Parker said. 'I've got a report to write.'

'Twelve,' Barbara said. She put the phone down and went to him and kissed him. 'How was I, darling?'

'Fine,' he said, but he gave the word an empty sound and looked away, as though none of this had anything to do with him.

'I'm hungry,' Barbara said, and studied the Room Service menu, then called the number.

Parker listened with detachment, and yet in his chair he had the sense of being on the brow of a hill, with a long shadowy slope beneath him ending in a darkness like a black lake piling little waves against the near shore.

'Hot pastrami and cheese on rye,' Barbara was saying into the phone. 'Cole slaw. French fries and coffee with two sugars.'

'Make that two,' Parker said.

6

WRITING the report about his idea for acquiring the sweatshop site didn't help. It only made him hate his work and despise himself for doing it. And he knew what he was leaving out, he was aware of his distortions. The very phrases he was too afraid to use were stuck instead in his mind. Now there was only one thing to think about.

His memory gave him glimpses of a woman tied to a chair and wearing a dancer's red dress. She was smiling, and then she was protesting – her eyes very wide, bulging when her mouth was covered with a gag. He smelled her excitement and then the sourness of her terror. Soon it was all confusion, and Parker had to shake himself free of the sight of it. Yet he knew – not enough to be sorrowful but enough to be sad.

He did not have a name or a word for any of it. He wondered whether he had imagined it. He remembered it as the day he was almost killed by the bus – when he had been meant to die, but hadn't.

Who was there to ask? But surely he had imagined it – he knew he was not violent. It was a misunderstanding. Perhaps he had just wished it into his mind, and now he could wish it away. But what was the truth? He knew he would be a failure until he knew the facts.

He began reading the newspapers. There was nothing

in the *Tribune*, but the *Sun-Times* had an item with the headline 'WOLFMAN STILL SOUGHT IN MURDER PROBE', referring to a 'savage Southside killing', two short paragraphs. And 'Wolfman' – was that him? He continued to read the papers, in the hope that the Wolfman would commit another crime, so that he could prove his innocence. He looked closely, he watched television, he listened to the mutters on the train; he was not consoled by any of the violence in this violent city, and what he heard and read seemed unspectacular compared to the work of the Wolfman.

Writing solved nothing – it only made him anxious, and these days he found that with nothing to do and no desire to sit at his desk he became very hungry. His strict diet was no longer enough for him. The Room Service meal he had ordered at the Blackstone was the beginning of a different sort of eating routine, and food he had not touched for years he now ate all the time. He had eggs – fried, with the yolks in; bacon and buttered toast, slabs of ham. He drank milk and ate hotdogs off a cart, with sauerkraut crammed in the roll. He went back to Chinese food at the greasiest Cantonese slop-shop on South Wentworth. That was a good decision. He was often sick to his stomach – he vomited in the corner of car parks, where people had pissed, and it was all foul; and yet some of his anxiety left him. He ordered seconds, he had pie, he ate Rocky Road ice-cream, with assorted toppings, and he knew the pineapple chunks were from a can. It did not matter. The food was a consolation, and who was it who had said, 'I love Chinese food – slurp-crunch, slurp-crunch'?

He did not ask his question aloud because he feared the answer. What pained him most was that the truth was probably very easy to find. He wanted it to be difficult, but he also wanted to be vindicated. And so he began his search.

It had to start with Sharon. He remembered her address from the way she had told the taxi driver, 'South Blue Island Avenue, at Throop'. What if it were all imaginary, a result of fasting and starving – and there was no night, no girl, no red dress? He wanted to know. Perhaps there was no apartment house at that address.

But there was – an eight-storey oblong of brown dusty brick and peeling window frames, with a horribly scarred doorway spray-painted with large initials, as though some savages had laid claim to it. There were steel grilles on all the lower windows. Parker had not remembered any of this. It was the middle of the afternoon and if she existed she would be at home.

Parker had left his car three streets away, at South Water Market, where some cops were clustered. It was a bad area and he feared for his expensive car. He walked through the hot exhausted air, gladdened by the sight of unfamiliar buildings and wrecked streets, and thinking: *I have never been here before.*

There were no names on the bells, and the front door was so badly vandalized it lay ajar, the lock hammered off. The stairwell was sooty and dark and something in the air made his breathing hard – three flights, and on the darkest landing he almost gagged, and his eyes were stung by the dust. There was no name here either.

The door was painted black and a dim bulb dangled from the pressed tin ceiling.

What did it matter if a crazy frightened woman swung the door open and accused him of assaulting her? At least then he would know the truth. He wanted her to accuse him – even to make a scene, to punish him for intruding – to be alive.

The bell rang inside, more with a rapping than a ring, and the sound of it made the interior seem huge and hollow, the echo in the empty rooms. He tried the bell a second and third time, imagining the rooms from the echoes, and only then did he see that the door was heavily padlocked. No one was inside. Perhaps she had moved? Perhaps he had the wrong door?

His insistent rings had roused a neighbour, and another door on the landing opened – not wide, only enough for the large loose face of an old woman to be visible. She wore an apron, her hair was wild, she looked hot and frightened. She turned slightly and Parker saw she had a hump behind one shoulder, and she stood hunched and lopsided, and began to close the door with her big mis-shapen hands.

'I'm looking for the woman who lives here.'

He gestured to the black door and the padlocks.

'She's not there –'

Hope enlarged Parker's heart and strengthened him, because *she's not there* meant she was simply out.

But the woman's halting voice was still audible to him through the narrowing opening of the door.

'She's dead' – and the door slammed shut and took the light with it.

Parker rushed outside to the bright street and thought *I am dying.*

He did not go home – he couldn't. He would be uneasy in the presence of Barbara, and anyway there was nothing he wanted to prove to her. And the baby would disturb him, Parker would not be able to hold him properly, he'd squeeze him and the kid would cry. Mother and child seemed to fill the house: you either saw them or heard them the whole of the time.

He suddenly needed Ewa, who was a stranger. He wanted to show her that she had nothing to fear from him. He believed he had frightened her in the parking garage, and more than anything he had to reassure her. If

I can't do that, and soothe her, he thought, I deserve to die.

'I'd like to take you out to eat,' he said into her answering machine. 'I'll call back in an hour.'

He had gone back to the Loop and was still there, wondering whether he should go to his office. He walked instead, in the shadow of the El, and bought the evening paper and searched it for mentions of the Wolfman. There was nothing. He was appalled trying to imagine what a murderer had to do to earn the name Wolfman.

And he wondered what Ewa would say if he asked about this murder. She would be spooked by his bringing it up. You could tell just by the way it had been mentioned that it had been a horrible crime that was on everyone's mind – all the readers knew the details, but why did they know more than he did?

He was reminded of certain details as he walked, but that was worse, because they were ugly in themselves – they had a strange shrivelled quality, as though they were decaying in his memory. He remembered the battered front door, the dead air in the stairwell, and they frightened him. Certain exaggerated words, the name Sharon, a woman's knotted clothes in a gutter, a girl on a bus with her mouth open and her head tilted back to reveal her throat, the sallow bundle of muscle and sinew and skin in her neck, a woman under a hairdryer looking as though she were being electrocuted, the memory of Mapplethorpe's violent photographs, the tricky pleading ads in the paper under 'Personal'. Anyone laughing seemed to be laughing triumphantly at him, and human voices made him feel desperate.

In a line to buy a 'Mr Misty Freeze' at a Dairy Queen he heard someone behind him actually say the word 'Wolfman' – a big angry woman speaking to her smaller woman friend, though Parker did not dare to look until a few minutes later. At the time he braced himself and believed that someone was going to twist his arms behind his back.

He tried Ewa again and this time she was in.

'I'm just going to the gym,' she said, as though he knew all about it and he believed that she had absent-mindedly revealed that she worked there, wherever it was.

'I've got to see you,' he said.

Her silence made him self-conscious, and he realized that he had said that same sentence to her before, and that she remembered it – but what had been the urgency that day? He no longer knew.

She gave him the address of the gym – it was on South Clark, near Burger King, blacks everywhere, and Parker bought a Double Beef Whopper with cheese. Eating it was his way of waiting.

Ewa showed up carrying a gym bag and dressed differently, in a sweatshirt and loose sweatpants, but wearing the same Reeboks. She said she had a class in *kenpo*, Korean martial arts – teaching kids.

'If you want, you can use the machines,' she said. 'They've got some good equipment here. I usually work out on that bench press. Do a dozen reps, maybe three or four sets.'

This was more than he had ever known about her. But he said he didn't have the right gym shoes, and he only watched – disgustedly, growing more annoyed as the hour passed, and he was angry by the time Ewa had finished teaching her class.

Had she brought him there and let him see her leading the class in kicks and punches and forearm chops in order to warn him? He guessed she had. But why? He did not need a warning from her when he was so frightened himself already.

Her skin was glowing from her shower, her hair still damp, as they left the gym. She said, 'I feel great.'

He wanted to tell her everything. What stopped him was the thought that she would ask him questions he couldn't answer.

Walking up Clark past the boys fooling on the sidewalk – perhaps they were trying to threaten them by crowding them this way? – he felt rattled and angry again, as he had at the gym.

He said, 'All these people exercising and jogging and lifting weights make me sick –'

He was surprised by what he was saying, and so was Ewa, but he couldn't stop – he was walking fast and still talking.

'Deep down inside they're bent, screwed up and morally obscene. It's so funny seeing these awful people taking their bodies so seriously.'

He laughed and the harshness of the laugh was more terrible than a scream, and Ewa stepped back and looked at him – he knew that look on a woman's face – as though he were a total stranger.

'There's nothing inside those bodies,' he said. 'It's just mindless muscle. That's why they're so dangerous.'

'*Kenpo* isn't fighting,' Ewa said. 'It's a whole philosophy. You could read up on it. I'd be glad to loan you some books.'

'It's fists and feet,' Parker said. 'I saw you.'

Ewa was still walking. 'I could put someone in the hospital if that's what you mean. If I wanted to. Hey, where are we going?'

'Here,' Parker said, seeing a yellow and red sign that said 'Hungry Tony's' and going inside. Instead of air-conditioning it had large whirling fans, like aeroplane propellers, that produced gusts of wind and blew napkins from the tables.

Parker had two kraut dogs and a Coke, and he encouraged Ewa to order a rib-eye steak.

He said, 'You can count on me. I feel there's been some sadness in your life. Some tragedy maybe. I could help you. Consider me your friend. You could ask anything of me —'

But what he said only seemed to alarm her. She was eating quickly, as though she simply wanted to be through and go home.

He said, 'Just remember you've got a friend. You're waiting to be made. I could make you. I'd like to see you happy.'

'You just saw me at the gym,' she said. 'I was happy.' She kept sawing small hunks of meat off the edge of her steak. 'I don't know why I brought you there.'

She didn't even realize that she had brought him there to show him that she was capable of putting a guy in the hospital with one of those sudden kicks.

'I think I'll have some ice-cream,' Parker said.

'So you eat normal food these days?' she said.

'I eat this food, anyway.'

Before Ewa said anything about wanting to go home alone Parker told her he would have to leave her, and she seemed relieved.

And when they were outside again he said, 'You've changed,' and he was convinced she had. She was not as funny as she had been, he thought. She was more serious — more earnest. She was suspicious of him, and not afraid, but evasive.

'Your office called,' Barbara said. It was nine o'clock. He was home. All he could remember of the drive to Evanston was his closing the windows and turning the tape-deck as loud as it would go — Verdi's 'Requiem'. 'They wanted to know where you were.'

Parker laughed — that harsh hollow laugh again,

attempting irony but expressing despair, his mouth open too wide, his tongue like a piece of meat. He meant his laugh to mean *I've been working all day!*

The laugh was the whole of his response. He said nothing because he knew that if he began he would tell her everything.

Barbara didn't question him. She seldom did. Now she was talking about the baby and about a new photographer she'd heard about.

Parker felt naked, as though he were a person whom anyone might get to know easily, and contradict, or abuse. He sensed that just outside his field of vision there was disorder, and that he was walking heel to toe down a narrow path. No one knew what he knew, so it was all up to him.

Her full name was Sharon Moser. The Skokie paper gave him details of her funeral – last Tuesday, at the Lutheran church. That seemed to make it so much worse – knowing her religion, hearing about the funeral service, learning that her mother's name was Ursula, that her father was dead, that she had a brother Richard, that she had been buried there in Skokie. So she wasn't just a solitary person in a room: she belonged to a world he had known nothing about. And it made Parker feel that he had interfered with that world, that he had upset the balance of it – that was the disorder, a lopsidedness, like the humpbacked woman who'd shut her door on him. The feeling sickened him. It was another hair in his mouth, with its tail tickling his throat, but this one he couldn't claw out.

St Peter's Cemetery in Skokie on that June day was very quiet and intensely bright and exposed, part of it like a quarry, he thought, and part of it like an obstacle course. It was no place to stroll in. It was for the dead to be disposed of, to be planted underground. What he saw bored him, and what he could not see frightened him.

He had trouble finding the headstone, and he realized why when he did find it – it was so small, hardly room enough for her name under her father's, just a length of granite, like a fragment of a kerbstone. Her name, not yet cut into the stone, was written in blue felt tip on the polished front, like graffiti.

Parker knelt down and began to cry. He wanted someone to see him and he didn't care if they reached the conclusion that he was responsible for her death. He hoped that he would be struck down by a thunderbolt – driven to the ground and killed.

The air was pleasant, though. A light breeze made the fresh flowers tremble on her grave; he had brought some in a cone of paper and inserted them into a vase with some wilted ones he did not feel he had the right to throw away. And then the wilted ones had more interest for him than the fresh ones – the way the petals had gone brown. He felt that he himself was weakening in just that way, going dead at the edges, and that he would be gone soon. He wept for Sharon and then he wept for himself.

He went quiet on the drive home, though he played the Verdi tape again. Seeing the peaceful orderly house, the empty rooms – Barbara and the baby were out – he burst into tears and could not control his sobbing. He was gagging and hiccuping, and in a grotesque way – like vomiting – it seemed to ease his sorrow, and he did not want to stop. He stripped naked and, still weeping, took a bottle of vodka into the bathroom and swigged it and choked on it. He continued drinking, sitting on the edge of the bathtub, leaning forward with his arms on his knees. He kept seeing the tiny grey piece of granite like a chunk of kerbstone. He wanted to drink and to sicken himself and die, but he was aware he was acting out a ridiculous melodrama. He wanted simply to be gone. He wished there was a deep hole that he could toss himself into and be smothered. But the alcohol was having that effect, of pinching his head and darkening his mind.

In this penumbra of drunkenness, he heard a sharp voice, and raised his wet face to the door. It was Barbara, demanding to be let in. He did nothing until she screamed at him, and then he staggered forward and unlocked it.

She was wearing lovely suedy-shiny shoes, light brown with dark brown trim, and fancy stitching around the toes, which were open. Her stockings were goldenish, with a repeated pattern of buds and leaves, and the hem of her skirt was soft, and shook slightly above her knees.

'What do you think you're doing?' she said.

He looked higher, past her breasts. He was frightened by her face. He knew that it was that way because she was looking at his face.

7

IT seemed that nothing was possible now, and after Barbara found him there in the bathroom, weeping and drinking – after he flopped forward into her arms and began chewing miserably on the shoulder of her blouse – he could not go to work. He knew why. In order to work for someone else you had to have access to another personality – the man at work, the boss, the employee. You became that other person when you sat down at your desk and wrote or opened your mouth in your office. You were that person there.

Now the man who did the work was gone. When Parker realized how Sharon had died, that he had murdered her, a hundred people died within him, a thousand moods faded, all those personalities in him vanished, and he was left solitary with a single version of himself. The dull fundamental man within him had never worked and he couldn't learn now how to adapt to it.

He sat and thought – but not about work. He kept imagining the women in the sweatshop, hearing their machines, the stitching sound like teeth nibbling cloth, and still chattering after the cloth was gone, as though murderously wanting more. And that young woman he had met on the landing. How she had said, 'billions', how she had said 'Sharon'. The thought made him tearful.

He was sadder and sorrier than he had ever known. This

stunned man was him, and had no disguises, nor any lightness. He could hardly speak, and when he tried his lips trembled and he was always afraid that he would weep, at first softly and then uncontrollably.

Then people would ask *What's wrong, man?*

They must not know.

Parker said he was very sick and he remained silent, while Barbara called the office.

'I'm afraid Parker's got a really bad bug,' she said. 'He's flat on his back –'

His being sick was her idea and she was so confident in describing his symptoms that he listened closely, hoping that she might be right. But what did she know? She was strong, and you needed strength to make explanations. He admired Barbara as he did Ewa, and he felt an obscure longing for them both and a need for them not to know him.

'You're burned out,' Barbara said. 'You need a long rest, darling.'

He stared at her from his low pillow, where his head had sunk in and he lay so flat he looked like a particularly serious casualty. He would not tell her what he had done. The burden was his: it was his guilt. It was unfair for him to try to ease it by making her share it. There was nothing she could do except weep with him, and he didn't want that. His own tears were bad enough. And murdering a young woman in a horrible apartment house late one night on South Blue Island Avenue after she'd answered one of his ads in the 'Personal' column? She wouldn't believe it. She would say *That's just one of your bad jokes*, which was what he had thought. And he had longed for that to be true – for it to have been someone else.

And the murderer *had* been someone else: that was what he had wanted to say to her. The murderer within him was gone, and he had abandoned Parker and left him to suffer.

Nervous breakdown was a wonderful expression, so helpful, and it meant nothing except collapse. That was the phrase that Barbara probably used when she was out of the house; it was probably what she told her mother. She used vague and kindly words for his condition. He was unwell. Even the doctor had said that – after she had tidied the house and put him to bed, and she had said nothing to the doctor about his being in the bathroom. *Stress*, the doctor said. *And remember that stress is an illness, just like measles or mumps.* Parker pitied the doctor and then hated him for his ignorant questions.

'You were confused,' Barbara said. 'You didn't know what you were doing.'

Which seemed to suggest that she felt very strongly that he had been trying to commit suicide, and he wondered whether this was so. But no – what good would his killing himself do? What he wanted was to restore Sharon to the earth: to give her life again. The beautiful, futile wish made him ache with despair.

'You were stressed-out,' Barbara said. 'Even the doctor said so.'

That made him think of a clock-spring wound too highly with its key, and it didn't console him.

'I knew that something was wrong,' she said. 'And I know what you need, darling.'

But she didn't know anything more than that he was in distress. He went to St Luke's: three days of being wired to machines and having a blood and stool check. *He's in for tests*, Barbara was probably saying.

'Sometimes it takes ages to find the source of trouble,' the specialist said.

I murdered someone, Parker wanted to say. *That's the source of trouble*. But that was no good, it was not enough, it wouldn't make him feel better; it would just make everyone else feel worse.

About a week after his discharge from St Luke's he was home, sitting in the living room's half dark, with the curtains drawn and bright slashes of sunlight showing beside the blinds and the glare knifing through.

'Do you know what I want to see?' Barbara said.

He sat idly, his arms very still and his palms upright, his hands like simple clumsy tools in his lap.

'I want to see the old Parker,' she said. 'His funny voices. His little skits. His crazy sense of humour. I want him back, to make me laugh.'

Parker smiled, and he meant his smile to say *Never*.

The man she talked about and wanted back was gone for good. That criminal had vanished and left Parker naked and weak. If he had not been so weak and drugged and lumpish he would have been terrified by her desire to have that man back. Parker was still smiling, and cautioning her with the smile. It was wrong to want things that you did not understand.

'I want him to make love to me,' Barbara said.

Parker saw the teethmarks on Sharon's throat, each bite like a mouth on her neck. She was tied to a chair, she was struggling as he tore at her with his teeth, mistaking her screams for eagerness, and blaming her for her desire, and – seeing her wounded – gagging her with her scarf, and finishing her off. That last bite when his teeth met in her flesh.

He was in agony when he remembered that, and what prevented him from telling her any of it was that he knew that she would pity him and not Sharon.

Barbara looked into his eyes and said firmly, 'You're going to be all right.'

He was so ashamed that she had found him in the bathroom, and he wondered what would have happened if she hadn't come home, if he had been left there. Probably this: him in bed, sick with remorse, but without the misunderstanding. Barbara seemed to think that he had wanted to be found, and needed her attention, and that by her offering it he would improve. She fussed over him. He was weak and slow and croaky, not like a murderer, but like someone with the flu.

It was odd that she should think his sobbing in the bathroom and choking down a pint or so of vodka had been a cry for help – something nervous and needy – when in fact it was the opposite. He had had only a vague sense of wanting her to be free of him, and his despairing wish to have Sharon back, so that he could be kind to her. It hadn't been a suicide attempt. He knew better than that. People thought they were safe at home but there was no criminal act that you could get away with in your own house – you'd always be caught there, and shamed at the sight of your sofa and your books and the photographs of your family propped up on the piano you used to play.

'Darling,' she said, softly, more tenderly, because he had started to smile again.

But he was smiling because he had just seen himself being handcuffed and led by two policemen past the photographs on his piano – the sweet one of his dad, his mother looking lovely, the skiing trip to Vail, his grandfather with a moustache, shaking hands with Harold Washington on the mayor's visit to the office, Barbara's folks, the hideous one of her mother Herma, Eddie's first portrait at three months. The Wolfman at home was a guy with an infant son, a Beemer, a mortgage and twenty framed pictures on his piano. *Isn't that the guy that used to be mayor?* one of the cops would say.

Barbara could be so tricky and childish and obscure. It had something to do with her having been born beautiful.

89

A woman with her looks had never had to be truthful. He hoped she would not suspect him of having committed a murder, but if she found out she would still be on his side. In her eyes it would not be a crime but a humiliation. His worst fear was that the police would find out – but he was not afraid for the usual reasons.

He imagined it: no penalty, only a fixed procedure, a sort of ceremony. After a polite arrest and thorough investigtion there would be an arraignment, a trial, newspaper coverage, the usual thing – 'Wolfman's Yuppy Lifestyle'. And he'd get life, meaning fifteen maybe, behind one of those slit windows in the tall yellow prison in the Loop. That was like slowly bleeding to death, but so slowly he would hardly feel it. It was nothing compared to the remorse he felt – the iron spike in his heart that was growing rustier by the day. Prison was no punishment; he needed something hurtful and drastic.

His sorrow took away his voice, and he gagged when he tried to speak. And sorrow killed his appetite, too. He hardly ate these days. But Barbara kept at him to eat, and her persistence, her mentions of food, gave him a sick disgusted hunger. It was a craving not to eat but to vomit.

'Get me some chop suey and fried rice and pork strips,' he said. 'And Oreo cookie ice-cream for dessert.'

Barbara laughed and looked pleased, as though Parker had at last recovered his sense of humour. But when she saw he was serious she became alarmed. He insisted on the food. She bought it, and she watched him eat defiantly, like someone taking poison. He made himself a milky coffee afterwards and filled it with so much white sugar that it turned to syrup in the bottom of the cup. That night he called Arby's in Evanston and had the menu read to him slowly: he sent Barbara for a Super Roast Beef with Horsey Sauce, potato cakes, a cherry turnover and a Jamocha Shake.

He had eggs the next day for breakfast, frying them in sausage fat, and he ate them with buttered bread and bacon rind and whole milk. He ate Danish pastry and fried chicken and Devil Dogs. He discovered revolting cakes with silly names like Yoohoos and Yodels, and he crammed them into his mouth. All the while he thought remorsefully of Sharon. He made the eating of Whoppers and Quarter-pounders into something like a sacrament.

The result after each meal was predictable enough, and his nausea – that tearful retching – was like grief, like another kind of sorrow.

The Chicago heat continued to saturate the days, and it affected him, like another symptom of his illness, driving off whatever thought had collected in his mind and making him forgetful. But one thing he always re-membered, his guilt, the poor young woman's corpse dead and stinking in the ground, and remorse making garbage of his heart.

On these hot days the simplest effort made him weary, but he felt a need to leave the house and for a week or more he had felt an urgency to see Ewa. Sometimes it seemed as though he wanted to impress her, so that she could testify to his good character. It was not that he wished to deny his murder but only to assert that he had never harmed her; that he was capable of better. But it was also the fact that there was no one else, and that for a reason he did not know he could only bear himself when he was with her.

He called her in the usual roundabout way, leaving a message, calling again later, and arranged to meet her at a neutral place. Was she married? Was that it – that she didn't want her husband to know? He hoped it might be true, that she had a secret life, and not just that business at the gym, because he had kept so much from her.

'What about the picnic area near South Lagoon,' Ewa said, explaining where he would be able to park, and the best exit.

She said it wouldn't be crowded, and she was right – she knew the city well. She was there early, before him, with the buildings looming behind her. She smiled when she saw him approaching, taking him in, his feet, his face, making him feel self-conscious. Her smile remained fixed but all the life behind it slipped away and she became doubtful.

She said, 'Are you in trouble or something?'

'No. Just lost a little weight.'

Yes, I'm in trouble, he wanted to say. *And it's all my fault*, so that she would see his predicament and not ask any further questions. But it was not possible. After you told someone that something was wrong, there were questions.

'New shoes,' he said – they were red and black Reeboks.

'I wondered whether you'd notice.'

Her saying that made him realize sadly that she thought of him when she was alone. He had seen her kicking aggressively in her *kenpo* exercises – had she called them *kattas*? She always mumbled, she talked too fast. He thought of her as very strong, but that way of speaking made her seem unconfident. And walking behind her on the path around the lagoon he thought how weak she really was. Anyone could smash her skull with a hammer, anyone could break her bones with a bat. She could so easily be jumped. Because he knew that, he wanted to protect her.

'You're never in any hurry,' she said.

Was she talking about his interest in her?

'It's because half the time I don't know what to do,' he said.

She dropped back to be beside him, and she said, 'I wonder whether you'r really serious. I mean, are we getting anywhere?'

'I'm so serious I want us to take our time,' Parker said. 'I'm crazy about you.'

'There's something I've got to tell you,' Ewa said.

He knew from the urgent way she said it she had something to confess – not just tell him but reveal to him. It took her a while to begin. She was still swallowing and looking away at the paddle boats in the lagoon.

'That personal ad you put in the paper,' she said. 'That letter I wrote – I've never done that before in my life. I still don't know what made me do it.'

'You were lonely,' Parker said.

'You've got to be worse than lonely to get into that,' she said, and she stopped – too tactful to go further.

She was right. It was a kind of sick desperation that drove people to it – he knew that better than anyone. He remembered the ads he had placed, his care in inserting the right clues, how there were certain words that worked magic, as the best fishermen knew that it was the type of bait that determined the fish. A suggestion of money worked with some people, or pleasure, or pain, youth or age, or any intimation of a door opening to a new life, or the mention of travel, or the idea – this never failed – that this personal ad was a first attempt.

Ewa sounded ashamed that she had replied, as though she had something to explain or apologize for. Most people said *I've never done that before* – never advertised, never answered. They were lying, but Parker believed that Ewa was telling the truth.

She thought she had done something strange and out of character, and she didn't want him to misunderstand. Yet in bringing up the subject she was the one who was vindicated, by her very innocence in mentioning it, and he was incriminated by the memory of more than a year of placing ads and replying to the needy and selfish letters that people sent. And their photographs – taken in four-for-a-dollar photo booths and in back yards or in streaky glary Polaroid shots in which they had red eyes and corpselike skin. What was saddest of all was that they were doing the best they could, and Parker hated his snobbery in finding them ugly and repellent. He had sometimes wanted to hurt them for being ugly, believing that their ugliness meant they were dangerous. But not Ewa – Ewa was the exception. Even she knew that.

She put her arm around him in a playful way and tugged the hair on the back of his neck. Parker became tense and walked off the path, with Ewa following. They sat under a tree, on the grass, side by side. Parker felt tender towards her, but didn't touch her. This knoll was high enough to give them a sight of the lake. Parker wished that the water were in motion. There was no wind, and the lake seemed shallow – big, blue, inert and inch-deep.

She slung her arm on his shoulder, as though she were the man and he the woman.

He said, 'God, if you only knew how I needed you.'

Ewa leaned over and looked at his face. He was still staring at the lake. She smiled and kissed him lightly. He jerked his head aside, but became self-conscious and turned and kissed her, pushing his mouth against hers, and gasping through his dead lips.

Her arm kept him from moving. She sighed and lay against him, and he was shocked when she slipped down and lay her head on his thigh. He was surprised by the weight of her head. It was so solid that it numbed a nerve in his leg.

They stayed that way for a while, her head holding his leg down like a stone; and then Parker suggested they continue their walk.

Parker sensed that people – passers-by – stared in his direction without seeing him: that he did not exist. He was afraid for these people, because they couldn't see him. And he was ashamed to be dressed as he was, in an expensive shirt and summer trousers and new shoes. These clothes, he knew, were no more than an elaborate costume. He wanted to be seen and known and naked, and he hated himself for having committed by pure accident the perfect crime.

Could he undo any of his guilt by being kind to Ewa? Now and then, walking close to her, he was fearful, for wasn't it much worse that he was risking her finding out who he was? Yet against all logic, with an urgency like desire, he admitted that he needed that friendship, which seemed something more powerful than love.

They came upon a man with a tin pushcart selling hotdogs. Parker bought two for himself but refused to let Ewa buy any herself. He tonged sauerkraut on to them and insisted that Ewa eat an apple. He bought one for her from the same pushcart, and when she polished it, pushing it back and forth on her sweatshirt buffing it against her breasts, he turned away and crammed the hotdogs into his mouth.

She said, 'You're still into junk food?'

He chewed and swallowed, feeling his gorge rise, and said, 'I eat what I want.'

Who said that?

Ewa was eating her apple slowly, turning it in her fist and watching him. She entered the underpass, leading him to the lake.

When she flung the apple core far out – so far Parker hardly saw the splash in the lake – Parker said, 'That lake has something to do with us.'

She looked at the still-smooth water that was greeny-brown and greasy at the shore and blue far out.

'I don't think about it,' she said, and shrugged like a little girl.

'The lake is always here,' he said. 'The rain bashes it, the wind blows off it and messes it up. It's huge. It's empty. It's more like a desert than a lake, always pulsing at the edge of the city. I love it at dawn when it has that hot red thermonuclear look. Then it turns black and comes alive.'

She thought he was making a joke, he knew that. She was thinking, *Of course it's not alive.* How could he tell her that he was trying to express something dramatic? He wanted to say that the lake was within him and that though it did have life it was not predictable, like a sea. It had no tides, it did not rise or fall. Not the buildings he had once worshipped, but the lake – its silence, its subtle colours – made Chicago Chicago.

He went silent again and thought: She doesn't even know that I'm talking about drowning.

He decided that she had the shallow selfishness of someone who would go on surviving, and yet there wasn't much vanity in her. She was quiet and composed in a way that proved to him that she wasn't very bright, and now and then, with a simple question, she reminded him of how little she knew.

'So what about that guy,' she asked, 'that monster in your office?'

'What guy?'

'That's into women's underwear.'

There was no guy, there was no office – she didn't know that he had killed Sharon, bitten her to death – he, the Wolfman; that he had been sobbing in his bathroom and his wife had found him and treated him like an invalid – didn't even know he still had a wife.

'He died,' Parker said.

'Oh, God.'

Her reaction startled him. Sometimes these casual lies were the harshest, the cruellest; he was sorry as soon as he said it.

'Don't be sad,' he said. 'It's much better. He was in terrible shape, although he thought he was really healthy. He was dangerous to himself and other people. It had to happen. Apparently, he was wired –'

And talking to Ewa about this man who had never existed, Parker felt that he was at last making sense; that this coherence was a result of the sympathy and friendship that bound him to Ewa, and that he did not want to leave her.

The afternoon grew hotter and heavier with oppressive haze, and just for the sake of the air-conditioning they went to a movie. She chose it, a Polish movie – not a recent one. It had a clumsy bleakness that gave it reality, and though it had white bleeding subtitles Ewa understood what was spoken before the words appeared. She reacted the moment someone uttered a word. It was called *Early Sorrow*. Parker wanted to leave almost immediately. Ewa wept when the girl in the little apartment was abandoned by the young man. Just the sight of that stone sink was upsetting.

It was a sad movie – everyone was sniffing softly. Parker wept too – and Ewa consoled him, rubbing her hard hand against his. She didn't know anything. He was weeping for what he had done.

8

For the first time ever, the Blackstone desk clerk was silent. It was as though the man finally understood, at a time when Parker had ceased to understand. Or did the man see misery and failure on his face, and pity him and leave him to himself? In any case, Parker regarded the clerk's silence as spookier than his questions had been, but he admitted that he deserved no better – he deserved much worse.

Barbara had told him not to worry. She seemed so sure of herself that he was alarmed, because he knew he would disappoint her again; and he wished for Ewa, who was never disappointed. He had agreed to a date because it was a new month, July, and one was overdue. But he was in despair: naked again.

Sitting in the room alone, watching the evening news, Parker was saddened to see there was no mention of Sharon's murder – no hint of a murderer on the loose, nothing on the Wolfman story. It was all politics tonight, the presidential campaign, and the little parcel of news people seemed to be gently mocking the exertions of the candidates. Parker had nothing but contempt for the news panel sitting behind the counter: the hard-voiced bitch, the fluffed-up fag in the blazer, the fat-faced sports reporter with his tie badly knotted, and the manic and unreliable-looking weatherman. There was a version of those four people on all the other news channels – more presidential coverage, more speeches, the same footage. No Wolfman.

Parker switched from aerobics to cartoons and back to the news, and found himself favouring George Bush. That was odd. A month ago his vote would have gone to the small efficient-looking Mister Dukakis. But what would Dukakis do about rising crime – not just Parker's crime (not traced, not mentioned, and seemingly forgotten), but crime all over the United States? Real punishments were needed for convicted criminals – something harsh. They had to be caught and punished so severely they would never harm anyone again. Dukakis was soft on crime: you could see that in his social worker's eyes; but Bush looked angry, and that was the right emotion.

Why not a dose of vengeance? Parker thought. All that happened to murderers and rapists in Illinois was that they were held in prison, in government-issue clothes, for a certain length of time; they had three meals a day, they had television, they had a recreation room, and most of them had access to drugs. Prison was no more than a simple room, like this one at the Blackstone, a light overhead and the same bare walls. John Wayne Gacy was in a room, Richard Speck was in a room – mass murderers played checkers and just let the time pass. They had no fears any more, because no one knew what to do with them. But now Parker knew.

He was still thinking *catch them*, *hurt them*, when 'The Love Connection' came on after the news. It was a dating show; he fingered the remote switch but he did not press it.

– *He had this real cute haircut and a real neat car, so I asked him to take me to Stradivarius, the disco near my condo, because it's real nice, plus I wanted my friends to check him out.*

– Did he kiss you?

– Yeah, sort of. No, really! He was dancing real close at one point and I liked the way he kissed, but he was wearing this really raunchy aftershave and he had tons of it on, and he told me about a million times –

Parker popped the button. *Porqué no?* a woman shouted in a Spanish-language soap opera, and she reminded him of the sweatshop on South Federal – the monkey-faced Hispanic girl with jet-black hair in a loose cotton dress made him so sad that he turned the sound almost off, so that the Spanish was a murmur. He watched the programme, feeling sorry for the women on it, not the characters they played but the actors themselves, perspiring as they went through the motions, and recited their lines, and shouted or wept.

The programme ended. He watched 'Jeopardy'. That ended. He switched off when he saw that it was nine o'clock. Why so late? He was hungry. Without looking at the Room Service menu he phoned and ordered a cheeseburger and french fries and cole slaw and a piece of chocolate cake.

– Anything to drink, sir?

'A glass of white wine.'

– We only sell it by the bottle or half bottle, sir.

'A bottle then,' Parker said.

The meal was brought to him on a stainless steel cart, the cheeseburger under a shiny metal dome, the cake enclosed by a lacy paper ruffle, the wine in an ice-bucket. The waiter pretended to be surprised by Parker's tipping him, and he left in an odd formal way, backing to the door and bowing.

Parker drank half the wine before he even lifted the lid on his cheeseburger. He had kept filling his glass – splashing it in – and sipping it. It was the first alcohol he had drunk since the vodka in the bathroom, and that vodka had been the first for seven years, when (as though taking monastic vows) he had started his severe diet. The wine gave him strength and helped the time pass and made him sadder. He switched the television on again, but when he saw a small dog cowering from its owner's anger – the big man was scolding the mutt – he began to cry, and quickly turned the thing off. By then the wine was gone, and so was the greasy food.

It was quarter to ten, and he was too drunk to find his way home. And it was late and dark: he began to pity himself for being alone in this little cell.

He drew comfort from the sight of the food cart he had reduced to garbage and disorder. Wheeling it into the corridor, he caught a glimpse of his tearful face in the mirror and went to the bathroom to wash it. He was pushing his face into a towel when he heard the knock.

'Who is it?' he asked. He genuinely wanted to know. His memory had been numbed by the wine, and in his loneliness and confusion he could not imagine who was knocking or what this person might want. When he saw it was a man he thought it might be a policeman. He simply stared at the man, with a wicked thrill, waiting for him to declare himself.

The man was slender, boyish-looking, with blue eyes, and already stepping forward as Parker opened the door. He was slightly shorter than Parker; he wore an elegant suit of light silky material, a white shirt and tie, and a panama hat. He seemed very cool and self-assured in these summer clothes. The man had fine features, he was smiling – but his smile did little to soften the face, because the lips were full – soft and selfish, and there was something cruel in the man's hard bright eyes.

'What do you want?' Parker asked.

The man stopped smiling then, for an instant, and moved past Parker without looking at him. His shoes were small and elegant; everything about the way he dressed spoke of vanity, and he glanced in the mirror as he went by it. From where Parker was standing, the man did not seem to have a reflection.

Shutting the door without a protest, Parker realized that he had surrendered and that he had allowed the man in – given the room to him and made a trap for himself. But he hadn't had a chance: the moment he'd seen the man's face at the door he was no longer in control.

The man turned warily like a cat, peering around, as though he had a tail that was swaying behind him, creating space, and then he sat. He seemed to claim the chair and take charge as soon as he was seated and still.

'You've been drinking.'

'No,' Parker said. 'I haven't.'

He regretted saying that, or speaking at all. Why hadn't he shrugged? It was none of the man's business anyway. The man's smile had come back. He knew that Parker had lied and Parker felt weakened by having been put on the defensive in such an obvious lie. The food cart with the empty bottle was in the hall with the single smeared glass!

'I'm expecting someone,' Parker said. 'She's late. Really.'

'Bullshit,' the man said – softly, mockingly, and crossed his legs and looked around the room. But it was more a sneer than a glance.

Parker was conscious of the smallness of the room – the way he was crowded by the large bed, the big television set, the protruding desk, the wide lampshade. He felt cornered by the man, and he moved awkwardly, looking for a place to sit.

'Sit down,' the man said. 'You make me nervous.'

He did as he was told – he moved quickly. The man's voice and his commanding manner – even the way he sat, with his hands quietly in his lap – excited him and made him breathless. He was frightened, his nerves drawn thin and tight like shrunken stitches. But that same thrill he'd had when the man entered the room had not left him, it had held him together, and made him lucid. He had no idea of what was coming next. Everything that had happened so far had been unexpected. What now?

The man frowned and said, 'It's stuffy in here – can't you turn the air-conditioning up?'

'No,' Parker said, and meekly explained, 'I've already tried.'

The man was watching Parker with those hard lighted eyes that seemed to penetrate the guilt and remorse in his soul.

'You're a secret drinker, baby.'

Parker shook his head and made a neighing noise, denying it, but he knew it was no use.

'What are you afraid of?'

'Nothing.'

Parker was sure the man knew he was lying – *nothing* was always a lie. But he was glad the man was so quick, and he was eager to know what the man would make of his fear.

'What's your name?' the man said.

'Never mind,' Parker said.

The man smiled again – a secure smile of power and mockery, and it panicked Parker into an alertness that was so keen he heard the dimmest sound. There was a scuffing on the hall carpet on the other side of the door.

'That's her. That's for me –'

The man had not heard it – did not believe him.

'– I told you someone is coming.'

'No one's coming,' the man said, defying him again with the jeering certainty.

They both listened and the next sounds were of the metal food cart being rolled away.

'You don't want anyone else here,' the man said. 'You don't want her. You're glad she's not coming.'

'Lay off,' Parker said, whining slightly.

'You're relieved.'

Parker stammered as he said, 'Get out of here and leave me alone,' yet he said it in a nagging and insincere way, as though to taunt the man.

And frightened by his own audacity Parker lowered his head – and he was thrilled again by feeling powerless. Parker shut his eyes and heard the man get up out of his chair – heard the lisp of the cloth chafing as he rose. The man walked over and stood in front of him. Parker sensed the heat of the man's body within his suit. He lifted Parker's chin, smacked his face lightly. Parker became intensely calm in concentration, as though he'd stopped breathing.

'I know what you want.'

'No,' Parker said, and gave himself away, because it was like an agreement.

The trousers were loose on the man's legs as he stepped nearer, his knees against Parker's knees, Parker's face level with the buckle on the man's leather belt.

'Open up,' the man said.

Obeying the man, Parker opened his mouth. The man put his slender finger into it and Parker sucked it, liking the way it filled his mouth, liking the loose skin on the bone; and he worked his tongue on it, wishing to please the man.

'You like that,' the man said. 'You love it –'

He did not have to reply – he was happier not being able to. He enjoyed reassuring the man, showing his pleasure by mouthing the man's finger and caressing it with his lips.

The man said nothing, and when he drew his finger away Parker blinked and looked up at him with imploring eyes.

'You want more,' the man said, and Parker slid from the edge of the bed to his knees.

An eager and pathetic *yes* lighted Parker's face as he crouched in submission. He turned away and lowered himself on to the dusty carpet between the bed and the chairs. He was on his hands and knees, like someone searching for something that he had just lost – something very small and elusive – with his face to the floor, and propped on his palms. He was at last where he belonged.

He was hesitant to take the initiative. He wanted to stay there on all fours, and he had the wild vivid desire for the man to mount him and penetrate him roughly, tearing him open, as though stuffing a furious rat head first into his hole.

He began to whisper, still with his head down.

'What?' the man said sharply.

Parker could not find phrases for his desire – too shocking, and what if the man refused?

'Do anything you want with me,' Parker said. 'Use me – use my body.'

The man nudged him and Parker lay on his side and then rolled over. The man was standing over him with the same towering indifference: he had not kissed him, he had been careless, he had hardly touched him. He seemed fierce, with his hat on, and wearing his jacket and trousers and beautiful shoes. The air-conditioner in the room gave out a harsh monotonous whine.

Parker was still fearful and eager, and his excitement still held him trembling. He was aroused – his cock was up and obvious.

The man said, 'Stay there – don't move.'

Even the coarsest command reveals the person's need, Parker thought. The man's urgency gave a note of pleading to his words, and that too excited Parker.

As the man kicked his trousers off, Parker pushed his own down in frantic anticipation. The man dropped to his knees and touched him and said, 'This is mine.' He sat on him and straddled him, enclosing him, and Parker felt he was being penetrated by that angry rat. The man showed his teeth and looked vindictive and growled above Parker's face.

'Tell me your name,' he grunted.

'No,' Parker said.

'Tell me.' He was sitting on Parker's cock and grinding him against the floor, and he was using his hands, his fingers to stab beneath him.

In a small tentative voice Parker said, 'I'm Sharon.'

The man grunted in satisfaction, and he said, 'You've never done this before, have you, Sharon?'

Parker was whimpering, feeling the weight of the man on him.

'Have you?' the man insisted.

'Never,' Parker said – in a child's voice, he was so completely in the man's power.

'But you love it.'

'Oh, yes.'

Enraptured, and vibrant, his body seemed to levitate and tremble, as though it was caught at the edge of a beach and was being struck and buoyed by a series of waves – struck and lifted and dragged down, and pushed and pulled by successive waves. He did not dare touch the man, but he hoped the man would go on holding him down and rocking against him.

The light in the room danced behind the man's hat brim, the ceiling was white above his square shoulders. But he was not heavy enough – Parker wanted more weight behind the man's thrust, he craved greater fear – he wanted to be flatter on the floor, pinned down so that he could not struggle. His pleasure was intense, and yet he wanted the man to spread him wider, to open him and wound him and split him in two.

The man was crying out but not in a man's voice; he had lost that and was like a child himself, a fierce boy. He was howling softly, a sort of audible darkness and heat issuing from his mouth, and in his frenzy his hat went flying and his hair shook loose and tumbled to his shoulders, great dark lengths of hair.

Awwwww, he cried, the sound leaking from his lips. He tore at his shirt and clawed it open to find his heavy breasts and finger his nipples. And then he was plunged into the privacy of his orgasm and it was both exaltation and collapse into a sudden revelation, like giving birth — to what? To a tiny harmless monster; and then he — she — was alone.

'Sorry, darling,' Barbara said almost sheepishly as she rose unsteadily to her feet, pushing her hair out of her eyes — but more than ever like a man in her unexpected apology. She adjusted her twisted jacket and shirt. There was blood on her inner thigh — a blackish clot and a smear, like a streak of jam. 'I guess I got carried away. Did I hurt you?'

Parker was still cowering. He was raw, he was sore, he was very wet; and now he remembered everything.

9

EVERYTHING the world had forgotten. The newspapers had stopped reporting it, the TV news talked
of nothing but the heat wave, the presidential campaign,
and the new floodlights for night games at Wrigley Field.
He, the murderer, was the only one who remembered
that violent death – how Sharon Moser had trusted him
to tie her up and how she had smiled when he turned
savage, and the way her whole body swelled, straining
against the knots and tightening them when he sank his
teeth into her neck and broke the skin and snapped at the
ragged flesh like a mastiff.

It had taken her so long to die that it enraged him, and
she was so badly chewed and mutilated that he had
quickened his violence, tearing at her, certain that she
would be better off dead. And he had the irrational
thought at the height of her suffering – as she had
helplessly slobbered into her gag – that she was guilty and
deserved it. He remembered thinking that.

Yet now, in the stark rationality of remorse, which
seemed to him like a fatal illness, he saw that he had made
her his victim.

For an instant, at the Blackstone, he had had a glimpse
of that same fear, before he had realized who the man
was – early in the encounter, when the man walked into
the room and took charge. It had been a continuous

frenzy after that and it had roused him. But it had not worked, because he had pleaded for pain and received pleasure – and he had never been in any danger.

He was unharmed, he was disappointed: that same experience could not be repeated with her. Barbara would never again dress as a man and visit his room and treat him that way. Her wicked inspiration had worked once, but it could not work again, except as a game of dressing up. Parker did not want to play a game: he wanted real fear, real pain, the sense of being trapped and victimized by someone who was wolfish and unpredictable.

'I've got a photo session,' Barbara said. 'I'll probably be having them all week. My mother will be coming for the baby. You can make your own lunch – there's some sliced turkey breast and salad in the fridge.'

She spoke these ordinary homely words the morning after she had dressed as an elegant young man and visited Parker in the hotel room and commanded him to suck her finger and finally sat on him, still wearing her hat and her necktie, and had a howling climax. Parker had not forgotten any of it, but it was gone for her – she had perhaps never taken it seriously.

'I'll take care of the sandwich,' Parker said.

'I'm so glad you eat that stuff now.'

'I like it,' Parker said.

He watched her dressing – first her panties, then her bra, and then her tights, and finally her blue dress. Each garment fitted her body snugly, holding it, enhancing it, giving it colour and contour; and then she wrapped her hair in heated rollers – never taking her eyes from the mirror – and combed it out. After that she put on her watch, her two bracelets, her rings, her string of pearls, and lastly her shoes. Light grey, they toned with her dress.

She sat and put her face close to the mirror and holding both hands to her eyes she began applying make-up.

'I've mentioned that funny woman Wilma, the assistant at the studio,' Barbara said, outlining her eyelid in black.

'Wilma with all the husbands,' Parker said, and he marvelled at Barbara's steady hand.

'She told me the strangest story about one of them. He was a little bit younger than her, an insurance underwriter, whatever that is, and he kept disappearing – going away every few weeks, on business, he said. But it wasn't business. Wilma checked.'

Barbara stopped speaking and leaned towards her reflection, concentrating on her make-up – she was now holding a tiny brush which she moved in delicate strokes against her lashes. And only when she had finished and blinked did she resume speaking again.

'It was another woman,' Barbara said. 'She confronted her husband with the facts – telephone bills, credit card receipts, all that stuff. And this is the interesting part: the man just brushed them aside and said, "This woman understands me."'

Widening her eyes and making a face in the mirror, Barbara then moved to her eyebrows – darkening the little ridges which had been plucked of all their hair.

'Before Wilma could say anything, her husband said simply that he had discovered that he enjoyed dressing up as a woman – wearing dresses and heels and jewellery and sometimes a wig. Wilma didn't know anything about it, but apparently this woman was into it in a big way and actually encouraged him. She showed him how to use make-up, she helped him choose the right clothes and they often went out together, like two bitches on the town.'

Barbara made fish-mouths at the mirror as she did her lips, and her expression gave a greater strangeness to the story in the way it distorted her voice.

'Wilma was shocked. "You wear women's clothes?" she said. She was disgusted and angry, and she told me she wanted to pick a fight with him. But her husband just left the room and he locked himself in their bedroom. Wilma banged on the door for a while, and then gave up. About a half an hour later, her husband came out. He was wearing Wilma's black evening gown, her pearls, her pantyhose, and his face was made up. Like this, I guess.'

She turned to Parker: her face was beautiful and bright.

'Before Wilma could say a word, he got her on the floor and fucked her brains out,' Barbara said. 'But she still left him. It wasn't the clothes, it was the other woman.'

Parker was looking for the face beneath the make-up.

'The thing is,' Barbara said, 'it's a hell of a lot more convenient when people are normal.'

'It sure is,' Parker said.

I'm a murderer, you're a tease, and as for *normal* what about last night? He felt isolated by his disgust.

'I think you're getting better, darling,' she said. And she drew away when he leaned to kiss her. She had simplified her face with this mask and didn't want to smudge it. 'You'll be back to work soon.'

He smiled a real smile at the absurdity of it, but there was no pleasure in this comedy. He was glad soon after when she left for the photographer's because his smile did not go away but rather petrified into a look of horror.

How little she knew. It was the reason for her energy. And the proof of her innocence was that she still believed in the future – a time when he would be well and working once more. He did not have the heart to tell her there was no hope.

The memory of their date frightened him. She had not questioned it, any more than she questioned the wild filthy words she sometimes screamed when they made love. They had never spoken about their dates afterwards

– never tried to analyse them – because only in that way could they continue meeting and surprising each other. All the thrill was contained in the unexpected and the unknown. 'Dates' was a neutral word. *Let's not give them a name.*

Once, long ago, before Eddie was born, she had shown up dressed as a Girl Scout, with braids and cotton socks – selling cookies. Parker almost fell for it, and then he went along with it, and the reason for this little girl outfit was that she was looking to be raped. Other times, as a nun or a nurse – or as another housewife looking for action – he had always been aroused, though he knew that dressing up excited her too. But last night, for the first time, as a man: had she realized that she had awakened remorse in him and given expression to it? He didn't think so. Barbara had counted it a success, though, he was sure, because she had aroused him. That was the only measure. But he was equally sure that he had revealed a need to her, and that the revelation of his weakness had given her power over him. Wasn't that the point of her story?

The memory of his submissiveness – on his knees, on the floor – made him ashamed. It was secret and stale, another dead thing that had begun to decay, a memory that made him even more remorseful. *What now?* he thought, because he understood Sharon better, and understood himself too – he had been startled and instructed – as though he had been flayed and cut open and showed the rotted organ inside his body.

Barbara's mother came at ten to take the baby. This woman was sixty-something, and yet her upbringing had kept her girlish. She was still very fat from her pleasures and appetites. Her name was Herma, though Parker had trouble saying it with a straight face and always uttered it doubtfully, as though it were one of those joky nicknames that didn't quite fit. Her father's name was Herman, and

Parker never saw her without thinking of her as a fat spoiled little girl with a kindly foolish father whom she idolized.

Answering the door, Parker saw her standing heavily on the steps – she looked so stout and top-heavy and uncomfortable in the heat. Yet how harmless and human she was – and how inferior he was to her. He wanted her forgiveness without knowing how to ask for it.

'Hello, Parker. Did Barbara tell you I was coming?'

She was hearty and nervous, she probably distrusted him. She was certainly uneasy with him, she didn't like him. Because of his diet – the old strict diet – he had never eaten her food: that had been like not listening to her or turning away from her. It was rejection. Her uneasiness made her overserious and sometimes unintentionally rude.

'Where is my little man?' she said, meaning the baby – speaking as though the baby could hear.

She's afraid of me, Parker thought. He sensed that he smelled rotten – that the foul odour hung over him.

Herma went for the baby, past him, up the stairs. When she came down with the child in her arms she was more at ease, she had something to hold, something to do – and now she had something to talk about.

'I'm keeping him for the day,' she said. 'We're going to have a wonderful time at Granny's – yes, we are!'

Parker was irritated by her nervous, mannered yakking, but she was better than he would ever be. She was not a murderer. He looked upon this woman as though on another species.

'Barbara said you're over the worst,' she said, pausing at the door.

I lured a woman out and took her to her apartment and tied her up and bit her to death. That was the truth. I am the Wolfman, and Barbara found me weeping in the bathroom and too drunk to make sense. But what had Barbara actually said?

'I'm feeling much better,' Parker said. 'I appreciate your asking, I really do –'

His sincerity seemed to baffle the woman. She turned for relief to the baby, and she said they'd have to get this young man something to eat, wouldn't they?

When Parker was alone in the house he went to Barbara's clothes closet and took out five dresses. He set them out, spreading them flat on the bed. He opened drawers and took out underwear – her silks had the weight and feel of liquid in his fingers, slips and panties like syrup. Her tights were soft and woven like spiderwebs. He loved the fringe of lace on one of her chemises, and the way the cups of her bras were stitched.

His pleasure was increased by his hesitating over these garments – they were so frail and insubstantial, and they hardly suggested the shape of a body. They took the shape and form of whatever filled them.

Parker drew the curtains and switched on the bedside lamp, itself a lovely thing with a lacy shade and forgiving light. Then he stripped naked. He pulled on a pair of black panties, and had to catch his breath. The moment they were on and clasping him he got an erection. The dresses didn't fit – he didn't have the waist. He tried one of the skirts but couldn't fasten it. Barbara had a satin robe trimmed with lace – French. Parker put this on, and her long-haired wig, and he walked back and forth in front of the long mirror.

How would it feel, he wondered, walking down the street like this, going to the station, sitting on the train? He could not bring himself to try it today. He walked around the house, he kept the wig on, he watched the lunchtime news. He put on lipstick and looked into mirrors – not full-face, but glancing obliquely at his reflection. Then he cleaned the make-up from his face and put the wig away. He took off the robe and put his own clothes on over the black lace panties. He got into his car and drove around Evanston, feeling the panties tighten against his skin. He looked at other women, not in a sexual way, but studying them, scrutinizing their clothes and the way they walked and sat and stood. It was remarkable what small steps they took, how they kept their feet together, how erect their posture was – and the effect of their posture on the shape of their breasts. And the prettiest ones kept their heads up and didn't slouch and hardly parted their lips when they spoke.

The men waiting at the counter at Wendy's did not look at him. He ordered a Triple Hamburger with cheese, a Frosty and a coffee. He felt conspicuous and yet no one saw him, even when he put four lumps of sugar in his coffee. No one cared. He expected the food to make him nauseous but all it did was make him weary and thirsty. He walked to a Dairy Queen and bought a Double Delight. He ate it, licking the spoon: no one noticed.

The label on the panties said *Wild Nights* – he remembered that later in the afternoon, in a bar, with men all around him. He felt confined by the black lace panties, he felt vulnerable. If any of those men knew what he was wearing they might kill him. He examined that thought and could find nothing wrong with its logic. He went home and reluctantly put everything away.

'You've been out,' Barbara said, when she came back.

'No,' he said, in a voice of gruff defiance.

She knew he was lying – but why didn't she care?

That was the first day in a week of dressing up. Each day he tried on different clothes, and one day – still dressed – he ventured into the car and drove to Skokie, parked at the hospital, drove to the cemetery, drove to a bar. But he stayed in the car, and he kept the doors locked. He never felt more naked than when he was dressed in women's clothes.

He had pretended with Barbara that the date at the Blackstone had been a game. He was nervous that she knew so much, and since they could not repeat what they had done, what use was it to either of them? He found himself being more masculine when he was with Barbara – after he took her clothes off and after he hid the new underwear he had bought for himself at the Wild Nights shop on North Michigan, and when he had scrubbed the lipstick from his face. He swore and argued and threw things around and slammed doors, and he hated this strutting, posturing maleness, because it reminded him of himself at his worst.

IO

I N this mood of secrecy he needed Ewa all the more –
and it had a strange and unexpected result. Feeling
vulnerable and feminine, as Sharon must have, he noticed
that Ewa was easier with him and more responsive.

She took him back to the gym, but reluctantly: he
could see that she didn't want to be responsible for
him. He worked out with her, and though he made an
effort he seemed half-hearted – he was short of breath,
and podgier, paler, almost bosomy from the junk food
he had been eating for a month. The food tired him
and made him nauseous and headachy; he woke in the
middle of the night, feeling his heart pound. Junk food
was salt-sweet and he was always thirsty, and what he
drank was also salt-sweet. He knew he had greasy
blood. This was how Sharon had felt every day, sort of
sick and stupid.

The gym only made him feel worse. His slowness
inspired Ewa and made her competitive. Side by side,
they lifted weights, did sit-ups on the slanted board, or
twisted on the machines. They compared numbers, but
Ewa's were always higher than his.

'You're having trouble getting it up,' Ewa said.

Parker's face was damp and sorry-looking as he turned
to her, and hers glowed with health. She wasn't even
winded.

117

'It's just an expression,' she said, but she was pleased that she had stunned him.

After that, he stayed out of it altogether. Violent exercise sickened him. Limp and dizzy, he usually threw up afterwards. He felt better sitting in the gallery or on the benches, drinking Coke and reading the newspaper and admiring Ewa's dedication. He told himself that she would live a long time.

Her exercises always preceded the class she instructed in *kenpo*. Her kicking and bending and swiping with her arms roused him, and the *kattas* she performed – all the techniques done in sequence – transfixed him. He was surprised by her gracefulness, because he had always regarded her as rather clumsy, and this was like ballet.

He told her. 'That martial arts thing you do – it's like a dance.'

'A dance of death,' she said. 'Know how dangerous those kicks are?'

He liked that, it roused him again, and he imagined being stomped upon by her: flattened and hammered to death, because he trusted and needed her. She trusted him, too – seemed to feel safer with him. She stopped asking him where he worked and why he had so much free time. He asked her whether she were on vacation.

'No,' she said. 'I'm on nights.'

He was no wiser, but he felt that she would tell him where she worked, if he asked. She might tell him anything he asked. She was friendlier. But he asked nothing of her, and his passivity emboldened her and gave her energy.

It was about four days after he became a spectator at the gym that, leaving the building, he made his routine request that they get something to eat – and she surprised him by agreeing.

'What about Chinese?' she said. 'Do you eat that stuff? Chop suey? Foo yong hai? Pork strips?'

She was joshing him as though they were old friends. The work-out had made her hearty and confident. He loved her when she was like this.

Parker said, 'I eat what I want.'

'I know a place,' she said.

And when they got to it, Parker said, 'They'll think we're twins.'

His blue tracksuit exactly matched hers, even to the white stripes on the sleeves and the piping down the sides of the trousers. It was she who had encouraged him to buy it and a good pair of sneakers, and now this was how he dressed when he sat watching her and drinking Coke. His street clothes were in the small black bag he carried, but he hadn't exercised so why bother to change?

Ewa took his arm playfully and said, 'Yeah, you're starting to look like me. Especially in that suit.'

She led him into the Chinese restaurant. It was called The China Moon and it was on East 23rd Street, next to a much larger place selling bamboo furniture. It was little more than a storefront, with small wobbly tables and a sticky floor and gusts of steam issuing from the kitchen. Ewa took charge – chose the table, greeted the waiter, ordered the food. It was pork strips and black bean prawns and a fishball soup. They both drank beer, and after Parker had given up Ewa was still wolfing fried rice.

'Carbo loading,' she said. It was one of his old expressions. She smiled. She had grease on her lips.

'You look happy,' he said.

'Because you've stopped saying what shit this kind of food is. I mean, I thought you were hassling me.'

'I like this food,' Parker said.

'Same here.'

'It's not shit if you like it.'

She squinted at him. 'Is that supposed to be deep – like, philosophical?'

She had a low appreciative laugh in which there was no hint of darkness. He marvelled at her power over him: she was very strong and she had perhaps just realized it, or realized his weakness.

Unzipping her tracksuit jacket, she threw her arms out and yawned. Her tee-shirt said, *Bad to the Bone*.

'A friend of mine got it for me in Panama City,' she said, when she saw Parker smiling at it. 'That's in Florida. The panhandle. Right on the Gulf. It's a beautiful beach – she said the sand's like powder –'

Parker had never known her so talkative.

'I live right near here,' she was saying as he paid the bill and stuffed the wallet into his tracksuit jacket. 'I've got an apartment on Cottage Grove.'

'I'll walk you home,' he said, because it seemed as though that was what she was hinting at.

On the street, walking in the early evening heat, she was again leading, taking the initiative. She told him that he seemed different. On Indiana, waiting for the light to change, she said, 'Tell me a joke,' and he became very sad.

He wanted to say *I'm a murderer*, but why should she have to share that terrible secret?

'You might as well come up,' she said, because he was hesitating at the front steps of her building, and a group of black men took an interest in his indecision – the way he went halfway up the stairs and then down again. Or was it the fact that their tracksuits were identical – unstylishly the same? Whatever, she took his arm again and led him up.

Her apartment – three rooms, if that – was rather messy but had a stacked-up look, as though she had made a sudden attempt to tidy it. Parker was touched, seeing several plants in the kitchen, thinking of her watering them. She found a beer for him and she poured some vodka for herself. They sat side by side on the squashy sofa, listening to the shrieking on the street below.

'It's so peaceful here,' Parker said.

Yet it was noisy, hot, airless – the small rooms stifled him. He had wondered what she would say if he told her it was the opposite of what he said it was.

She unzipped her tracksuit jacket and took it off. She was still wearing the tee-shirt. Parker did the same in a companionable way, throwing his jacket over hers.

'It's not bad,' she said. 'I grew up on Milwaukee Avenue – where else? But I wanted to get away from there, live on my own, be a little independent. I still see my folks. They hate it down here. I mean, this is the jungle as far as they're concerned. But I can look after myself.'

She put one arm around him, and raising herself against him she made him seem small and in need of protection. She hugged him gently and comforted him.

'You don't know me,' Parker said, and wondered what he would say next.

'You think you know me?' she said.

He shook his head. They were both still strangers to each other, and it was as though they wore layers of clothes.

'I've kept you waiting,' she said.

Parker protested, but she hugged him again and calmed him.

'I mean, no romantic evenings yet.'

That was the phrase he had used in his personal ad; she had not forgotten it. He was ashamed – more than ashamed, he hated the thought that he had plotted in that way to gain her confidence. *Loop Exec* he had called himself. Horrible, horrible; because it made him remember the other ad, the other date, and how it had ended. How carefully, how creatively he had written

121

those personal ads, with all the loaded words winking in those few lines.

Ewa had not noticed that he had been struck dumb by her quoting his ad. She was still talking.

'– only if you understand where I'm coming from,' she was saying. 'I got really hit on by a guy once.' She fell silent, and when Parker said nothing, she added, 'Really hassled.' Still Parker did nothing but stare – he was staring at the little image of the personal column. 'I mean, raped,' Ewa said.

He heard that. 'Oh, God,' he said, and pushed his face against her. He did not want to hear more.

But she moved slightly, and reached for her drink. Sipping it, she said, 'I even knew him a little. He was a scumbag. He's in Joliet, doing time.'

In his rising anger, Parker detached himself from her and sat forward, seeming to grow larger. Fury concentrated his mind and a shadow – it was the blind black shadow of outrage – was thrown over his memory. He could think of nothing now except the hideous injustice of this lonely woman's ordeal.

'That's horrible,' he said, and startled her.

'I was in counselling for a while,' Ewa said quietly, seeming to see that Parker was upset and needed to be calmed. 'They said I needed to deal with it. I needed to grow. I had to move on.'

'You mean, forget about it?' Parker was still crouched like a monkey at the edge of the sofa. His nerves sang with fury – he kept clasping his hands, couldn't hold them together. 'Just like that – forget a guy raped you?'

'Forgive and forget,' Ewa said. 'That's dealing with it. Don't let it haunt you, I guess.'

'Are you shitting me?' Parker said. 'Forgive this fucking monster who did this thing against you. What good does forgiving do?'

Ewa started to answer, something about dealing with it, not letting it haunt her, but Parker's voice was a low roar of indignation that overwhelmed her.

'A crime was committed against you. An adult male did it, broke the law – probably injured you physically as well as mentally. Nothing can undo that fact.' He had begun to stutter and spit. 'No forgiveness! He should be punished!'

'He could have got zip to ten,' Ewa said. 'He got five. He'll probably do two, tops.'

'You said you knew him?'

'I knew who he was,' Ewa said. 'I knew his fucking name. He didn't think I'd report him.'

'But what good did it do – the sentence is pathetic,' Parker said. 'He's sitting in the prisoners' lounge watching game shows.'

'So what do you think he should have got?'

Parker was trembling, and though he knew his anger had alarmed Ewa there was nothing he could do. He felt hot and indignant and violent, and he pitied Ewa, because he believed that she had not known that man at all, because she had been tricked. But Parker knew the man well and could have told her all about him.

'He should be raped,' Parker said.

'Jesus,' she said, and seemed genuinely shocked, because Parker's eyes were fixed on hers.

'Over and over,' Parker said. 'Make him eat it.'

'He'd eat it now,' Ewa said. 'After the counselling I took up martial arts. I got interested in this Korean one: *kenpo*. I had a Korean instructor. The whole thing is very oriental. You probably noticed the way I bowed and stuff.'

Parker heard a note of revenge in what she said, and he was consoled, because he knew she was strong.

'This is lethal,' she said, showing him her pretty hand. 'I could kill with this.'

But she touched him softly and drew him back against her, and she held him, as though comforting him. She knew that what she said had affected him, and though she was probably glad that he had shown such fierceness on her behalf she was disturbed by the words that Parker had uttered. *He should be raped* had made her wince. She seemed sorry that she had told him.

They breathed together for a minute or so, Ewa still holding him, but more like a mother than a lover.

'I have to go pretty soon,' he said.

'What makes you think I want you to?'

She sipped her drink again, then wiped the wetness from her mouth with the back of her hand, and snuggled nearer to him. Her fingers snaked across his leg and she touched him lightly with her fingertips.

'I can't let you go like that.'

What did she mean? Her hand was massaging him as she searched his body. But there was nothing for her to hold, and he edged her hand away, cautioning her. He was limp inside his black Wild Nights panties.

'I'm probably drunk,' he said.

'Then you're in my power,' she said. It meant nothing. It was just something else that she had once heard.

He was glad when she kissed his cheek in a certain way, her nose against him. It went with the way she had held him a little while ago. It was a mother's kiss, familiar and affectionate, a touch of her lips, without anything behind it – no question, no demand. He was certain of that, because he had known so many kisses that came from starvation.

'Don't bite me,' Parker said, in a teasing tone that saddened him.

Ewa drew back from him. She looked at him closely. She said, 'I'd never do that.'

'I was just joking.'

'Jesus, what a joke,' Ewa said. 'You know, one of the worst wounds you can get is a human bite? Even if there's the least suspicion that someone broke the skin you need about fifty shots, plus observation.'

'How do you know this?' Parker said.

Ewa seemed very uneasy, and Parker became eager: what did this mean to her?

'I just know,' she said. 'It's one of those things you have to know. If you don't know it I feel sorry for you, because I figured you were bright.'

Parker put his hand on her and she recoiled again and squinted at him.

'This guy I know from the gym took me aside one day and lifted up his shirt. "Look at this," he says. Bites all over him – on his chest, on his back, on his neck. He yanks down his sweatpants. He's got bites on his leg. I says to him, "You look like dogmeat."'

Ewa was shaking her head and smiling in disbelief, as she must have done at the time, Parker thought.

Parker said, 'Maybe he liked it.'

'"I guess I got lucky," he says' – Ewa wasn't listening. 'He picked up a woman at a place called Eddie Rockets. He brought her over to his place and, somehow, she bit him. All over him. He says to me, "I guess I pushed the right button."'

Ewa put her arms around Parker, she rested her head on his shoulder, she was tense again.

'The next day they took him to the hospital,' Ewa said. 'He had chills, a high fever, vomiting – they couldn't diagnose anything. He could hardly breathe. He turned pale, he couldn't eat. For about a week he was very low. They kept him on antibiotics and eventually he was back in the gym. Sure – I might bite you.'

Yet there was an intensity in the way she held him that was itself like a question.

'I'm not up to much,' Parker said.

'Then just hold me – hug me,' she said.

He did so, and her whole body seemed to sob against him, trembling as she took several laboured breaths. It was as though she were freezing and had clasped him and then was discharging these sobs and spasms into his body like pleading words, so that she could be warm.

But her clutching him had deadened him and made him feel like a stone to which she had attached herself: she was a loose live thing, simply holding on. Parker could not bring himself to respond. Ewa was thick and urgent with life, yet he was depleted – he felt he was empty. Everything was over for him, and he wanted to cry, to mourn the passing of his vitality. He had no sex drive, no desire to live, no hope, only sorrow for what he was and what he had done. He sat in this unanswering slackness, and her weight against him made his cock feel as insignificant as a piece of string: her body was a question to which he had no reply.

He wanted to warn her again, but he realized that any warning would only frighten her the more: she had been raped.

So he decided that he must leave, as soon as possible. He had been so eager to see her, and now he couldn't wait to leave. But it was all his fault. She was trusting and he didn't deserve her trust. He vaguely despised her for being with him at all, for not being more careful.

Mentally he was disentangling her arms, picking up his jacket, hurrying out of the door – down the stairs and into the street. He wanted so badly to be away. He still held her hand so that she would not fumble inside his tracksuit pants and discover what he was wearing.

'It's all right, darling,' she said.

She seemed to be talking to herself, and yet he drew comfort from the way she said it. She was asking nothing

– only the chance to hold him, to shelter against him, because he had been so passive. He could not deny her that, and in fact he reasoned that it was much more than he was entitled to: she was kind, trusting, unsuspicious.

At last, she said, 'Yes. If you want to go –' And she released her hold on him.

It had gone dark, night had fallen while they sat there on her lumpy sofa, and she had not turned on any light. He had become a lump beside her, and then he sprang up, fumbling for his jacket in the darkness. But he hesitated, feeling grateful and sentimental.

'I need you so much,' he said. He had said it before, not knowing whether he meant it. But now he did mean it, and he was desperate for her to accept it, because he had nothing to give her. 'Do you believe me?'

Nodding in the darkness she shook the sofa and she made a sound in her throat that suggested that she might be laughing softly, wondering why he was trying to say any of this.

'Please don't give up on me,' he said.

She drew a deep breath, and sighed, and said in the silence that followed, 'I don't have anyone else.'

He could have said the same, but he felt that if he did he might overwhelm her. He said nothing, but he saw a chance for them: she had been a victim, so the way was clear for him. He had to offer her whatever he had; he had to serve her.

He said, 'I'm going to surprise you. Anything you want – anything at all. Just ask.'

It was his only salvation. And if she were really greedy, and used him, he might be redeemed.

'Maybe I just want you as you are,' she said, 'and for things not to change.'

He could not reply to this. He was on the verge of tears. He was glad it was still dark in the room.

'That's all I want,' she said, because he hadn't said anything.

She believed it was a simple wish. She did not know that it was the hardest wish of all.

He kissed her, he snatched his jacket, and he left, hurrying into the darkness. But instead of going home he walked north, up Cottage Grove, slowed by the heat that thickened the night air.

II

HE was so glad to be out of that place he kept walking, up Cottage Grove to Cermak and then north along Indiana, carrying his tracksuit jacket because it was too hot to wear it, even at ten on this summer night. He calculated that it was only a mile and a half to the Loop, where he was headed, to catch an Evanston train home.

The rhythm of his steps produced whole sentences in his mind, the ones that Ewa had said, *No romantic evenings yet* and *I got really hassled by a guy once* and *I don't have anyone else.*

Now he knew that she lived in a cramped apartment, she drank vodka, she wore blue jeans, she listened to the radio – and what a radio, held together with electricians' tape – and she probably worked in the gym. Now and then she looked at the exercise machines and muttered to herself *Do some reps.* Parker knew something else: that he had to help her, not to rid himself of his remorse, but because he owed so much to her. She had been kind and sympathetic, she had been unsuspicious, she accepted him, and after all this time it seemed that she desired him. He didn't deserve it. But how would she react to his help?

Turning derelict buildings into productive pieces of Chicago real estate had given him insights into transformation. Architecture was a cosmetic art, and it was a kind of religion in this city. But there was something heartless in the aesthetics of designing buildings. Parker had abandoned architecture to found High Impact and fill those structures with purpose and profit.

He wanted to turn Ewa into a North Shore property-owner, in Barrington or Northbrook, in a house with turrets and a trash compactor; the sort of Ravinia committee-woman a man didn't dare hit on, who didn't need a man. Parker planned to give her everything he had, just hand it over to her, so much of it that it would seriously inconvenience him. At first she would reject it – she would certainly laugh at him. She had always been evasive and hesitant. She would accept it eventually, when she understood what it meant. And he was not dismayed by the thought of initial caution: it had saved her the night he had killed Sharon.

There were men sitting on the front steps of the dreary brick apartment buildings on Indiana Avenue. Some of these men spoke to him – sort of heckling him but without much interest, like dogs barking, not at a man but at another dog. They were just reminding him they were there. He glanced up but he was afraid to meet their eyes. His sadness had nothing to do with the men. He was thinking of Ewa's impossible wish – *I just want you as you are, and for things not to change*.

It showed how little she knew. Yet he still could help her, he could be a friend. He owed her a great deal, after denying her so much – all the lies he had told. He imagined a relationship with her in which he made every sort of sacrifice for her sake – everything that he had failed to give Sharon he would offer to Ewa – life, freedom, wealth, happiness, anything she wanted. He would make a gift of the rest of his life to Ewa; he would save her. And she was perfect, because she had been victimized – she had been raped. There was nothing else on earth that he could usefully do: he wanted to be wrecked and for her to rise.

He had walked as far as Eighteenth on Indiana – they were long blocks here – when he saw a tavern. Its door was propped open, there were people inside, tough-looking people, mostly men. He went in. The place was poorly lit and crowded, drinkers standing against the bar, swigging from bottles; and it was hectic and hot: rock music playing on the jukebox, the television showing a baseball game, some shouting, and lots of smoke and talk. As Parker approached the bar a man turned his full face on him, and made room for him, and still watched with ponderous drunken attention as Parker ordered a beer.

The bartender served it quickly and messily, snatching the handle reading Draft Bud, plopping in beer and foam, spilling it as he slid it across the bar, and everything was dripping – the glass, the varnished bar, the bartender's fingers, the coins handed back to Parker as change, wet nickels and a slippery dime.

The man at the bar had not stopped staring, and he was also doing something subtle with his head – twitching it slightly, sort of haughty and incredulous.

'Is there anything wrong?' Parker said.

'Ornamental fish,' the man said, and glanced at the lighted aquarium behind the cash register. Parker hadn't seen it among the gloom of bottles on shelves and mirrors that reflected nothing except the shadows of the bar and all those men's heads. In the tank big bright fish darted or slowly rose and sank.

'Yeah, ornamental fish,' Parker said, and took a drink, wondering why he had entered the bar when he had been hurrying to the Loop to go home.

'You look real familiar,' the man said. 'Like someone I used to know. A very dear friend.'

He had spoken in a taunting way; even so Parker was touched that the man had spoken at all. He was a big fellow with short hair and a moustache. In spite of his size he was gentle, Parker could tell by his hands; he had a kindly face, too – but a humorous one, slightly mocking behind his moustache. He wore a loose blue tee-shirt and cut-offs and sandals, and yet his skin was pale. He worked in an office, he wore a suit all day, he wasn't what he seemed in this beat-up tavern, where the video games added to the racket.

'Do you live around here?' Parker said.

'Isn't it funny?' the man said, and put his chin in his hand and stared hard. 'People always ask the very questions they want other people to ask them. Get it? You never ask "Where did you go to school?" unless you want to say where you went to school.'

'I'm from Skokie,' Parker said, and felt threatened by the man's gaze.

'Sure you are,' the man said in a slow impish drawl, as though he were the one being teased.

Parker had been gulping beer and now the glass was nearly empty. The man noticed this and beckoned to the bartender.

'Two more,' he said, indicating Parker's glass and his own.

The noise in the bar was like thick smoke, but bolder and bulkier – it took up space and it seemed to give the man courage, because having made room for him he now stood nearer to Parker. He said nothing more for a while, but simply smiled through the music and the chatter.

With the knuckles on the back of his hand the man pushed the full glass of beer to Parker, and he came a step closer, seeming to follow behind the glass. There was something questioning in just the way he stood, a sort of challenge in his posture.

Parker instinctively looked down and saw the man's big pale legs and the light hair on his shins. His feet in rubber sandals were very dirty and they contrasted oddly with his broad pink face and his pale hands.

'I want to hear all about Skokie,' the man said.

And he did something with his shoulders, a mannered shiver and shrug that conveyed both affection and mockery – just the slightest gesture, yet its playfulness was unmistakable.

Parker said, 'I'll tell you later.'

This made the man laugh, but a bit too loud, and the overloudness excited Parker.

'I'm George,' the man said.

Parker hesitated, the man was staring, wanting a reply.

'I'm Sharon,' Parker said, feeling reckless and truthful.

The blue in George's eyes made them seem very weak and unfocused. He had not blinked, but he had softened his gaze as Parker said the name.

'That's a nice name.'

The man was next to Parker now. His rough look was an affectation – his short hair revealing his bumpy head and small ears. His voice was gentle. His teeth were white and even and rather small, and when he smiled Parker could see his gums.

'That's a very nice name,' he said, because Parker had not said anything more.

'Can I buy you a drink?' Parker said, raising his voice in the din.

George said, 'You can do anything you want, sweetheart.'

His voice was thin and scarcely audible, it had the pitch of a boy's, and when he tried to raise it against the tumult in the bar it was not louder but only shriller.

Parker waved to the bartender but could not attract his attention, and he was too timid to call out – to hear his own voice or for others to hear it. More than half the men here were black – they'd laugh at his voice saying *Excuse me*, or they would say something.

'I can wait,' George said, and glanced up at the television screen. Now it was showing one of the presidential candidates, wagging his finger. 'What's fourteen inches long and dangles between his legs?' George said, and hardly paused as he licked droplets of beer from his moustache and added, 'His necktie.'

The hurried way the man told the joke made Parker anxious: the same fearful thrill he had experienced when that elegant man had entered his hotel room, the same whiff of danger.

'Skokie's miles away,' George said, in the same teasing flattering tone of surprise. 'So what are you doing here?'

'Looking for trouble,' Parker said, the heat and noise in the room making him feel reckless. He was fascinated by the way his words brightened the man's face, those pale eyes, the lips nibbling and curling behind the moustache.

'You came to the right place, Sharon.'

'Two beers,' Parker said, because the bartender had returned.

'She's taking her time,' George said, as the bald big-gutted bartender filled the glasses. 'Never mind. We've got all night.'

Parker fished in his jacket, unzipped the pocket and pulled out his wallet. It was an odd size, but Parker did not question it – the strange feel of the wallet proved how drunk he was. It seemed small in his thick stupid fingers. George was watching closely, smiling, because Parker seemed to be having trouble with the wallet. When Parker flipped it open to get at his money he exposed a bulky silver badge fastened to the leather and the raised letters read very clearly *Chicago Police Department*.

'What the fuck are you trying to pull?' George said, his voice much shriller and womanish in anger. 'You're a cop.'

'No, I'm not,' Parker said and slapped the jacket pockets – there was nothing in them. He reached in a pleading way for the man who was still backing off. Anger and fear distorted his moustache.

'You're not busting me, bitch.'

Parker said, 'I'm not a cop –'

'You should get Aids,' the man said, still moving, before the music and the crowd closed over him. 'You should die for that.'

'Put your money away,' the bartender said. 'It's on the house, officer.'

Parker was fumbling a card out of the wallet. It was an official card with a thumbprint and mug-shot on it. It read *Ewa Marie Womack* and gave her address as Chicago Police Department, South State Street. There was a twenty-dollar bill in it and some singles, a bus pass and a Saint Christopher medal.

A stout man across the aisle on the Evanston train kept eyeing him. It was not the man's stare that bothered Parker, but rather his smile each time Parker glanced up. He imagined that this man knew everything: not only about the murder, but about Ewa, that she was a police-woman, and that Parker had just made a mess of things in a bar on the South Side; that he had been rebuffed by that man George, that he was running away – that he had seen him and knew he was a murderer.

He was a large tidy man with a bulging briefcase, and his necktie still knotted and his cuffs still buttoned. He got up and tottered as the train slowed at Dempster. There was something sinister in his neatness, and his stumbling made him seem malevolent as he came towards Parker.

'You've been working late,' he said.

The word *working* sounded sarcastic, and Parker did not know what to say.

'I haven't been working at all,' Parker said, and in that moment was not even able to say what his work was, where his job was. He had no work: he had no excuse at all.

'How's the school?'

'What school? There's no school,' Parker said, and felt miserable, being mocked by this man – was he crazy? Was he a jeering cop? 'I don't know you.'

The man positioned himself with his feet wide apart and pointed a finger at him. Was he drunk? He said, 'Yes, you do! Harry Baskies – waste management. And you're the principal.'

It made no sense at all. It was a trap, it had to be. Parker turned and saw there were only three other people in the car, half asleep in the late train.

'You had work done on your pipes,' the man said.

There was crude innuendo in this, Parker could tell by the man's accusatory smile.

'You've got the wrong man,' Parker said, but when he stood up to change cars and pushed past him, the stout man did not try to stop him. He merely looked surprised and sad.

Feeling rattled in the next car, Parker looked back. The man had not followed him and it was not until he was sure the man hadn't tailed him from the station – as Parker was walking home – that he remembered who the man was, from long ago: how that man had listened while he had pretended to be someone else, the high school principal. It was a reminder of his insane compulsion to deceive and dominate strangers any way he could and it was a glimpse of how dangerous and unreliable he was – a killer. Wolfman.

He was self-conscious, moving like an intruder – aware of his awkward feet and hands – as he entered his own house. He felt that he was clumsy, that he was someone to dread, worse than a burglar, more dangerous. It was not an extravagant notion: it was the truth. He knew he did not belong in this orderly house.

The lights were on: Barbara always left them on in the belief that bright lights kept intruders away. It was past midnight, she was in bed, and Parker moved uncertainly towards the stairs. It was just as though he had broken in – he had no business here. The lights found him and filled him with shame, and he turned aside from mirrors and wished he were in the dark.

He put the tracksuit jacket down, then thought better of it – picked it up and made a bundle of it and stuck it under his arm.

It was so cool and clean here. He had come from Ewa's stifling apartment, from the bar, from the confusion with that bewildered man on the dusty train that had hammered and clanged through the darkness. He was sweating, he was dirty, and he imagined that he smelled: anyone up close to him would know he was guilty of a savage crime that still stank on him.

He opened the bedroom door and stood awhile, just inside the room, until Barbara sighed and turned over in the bed.

'I'm sorry I'm late,' he said. 'I had a problem.'

A small sound came out of the darkness, a groan, a sigh – something from Barbara.

'Are you asleep, honey?'

'I was until you came in.'

'I'm sorry.'

'I heard you.' She turned again, thrashing the sheet. 'You had a problem.'

Parker could not speak. There were tears in his eyes

and his chin was unsteady, trembling. He knew he would cry if he tried to say something.

'I don't want to hear about it,' Barbara said, her voice falling as she seemed to sink into the bed, going back to sleep.

How could he sleep with her? He had no right: he was a stranger in this house. He backed away and went to the baby's room, where it was dark except for the tiny nightlight, a small bulb shining in a plastic lamp, with Mickey Mouse on the lampshade. The sight of it angered him. That was the new ikon, that cartoon. It was not wicked but it was very stupid, and something so stupid was dangerous. Mickey Mouse was God – the fatuous smiling creature consoled people, because it was not human and not an animal and did not threaten anyone. It was a toy and it was not associated with any particular age or region or country. Mickey was a universal symbol of acceptance, and so people worshipped it – this item of colourful vermin. The worst of it was that people turned away from reality to venerate it. They pretended not to take it seriously, but they held on.

Here in the baby's room it looked both devilish and innocent, and Parker remembered that he had bought it at the baby store in Evanston. Little Eddie lay in his crib, a small lumpy bundle, like a potato, his smooth white head showing. He was perfectly still, with a little shadow masking his face. The room smelled of his milky breath and talcum powder. The baby was frail, soft, pure, and knowing this Parker felt lethal and filthy – such a sense of self-disgust choked him that he stepped quickly back from the crib. Although he had just set foot in the room he felt he was already endangering the child, corrupting his innocence.

He moved to the door, sickened by the thought of who he was and what he had done. He was disfigured, his harsh breath was repellent, and he was disgusted by the clammy sweat from the Loop which still clung to him and which he imagined stank like poison.

Leaving the baby's room did not help. He hardly paused on the stairs. He went to the front door and left the house without looking back.

12

H<small>E</small> went into the dark: he felt bold and hopeless
– he had got a kind of courage from his aimless
sorrow. No one was worse than he, so he had nothing to
fear.

After he shut the door of his house and went away,
down the walk, beyond the hedge, he was alone with his
remorse. But instead of suffering it as he knew he deserved
he felt himself slipping away, collapsing under it. He
sensed that he was cracking and coming apart.

Sorrow and hopelessness were breaking him in two.
He could no longer remember who he had been. That
was a relief, but it disturbed him when he reflected on it,
for it was as though he had come from nowhere into the
world, and found it sad, and made it sadder. He looked
around and saw that he had created misery in the world.
He had once lived two whole lives and now there were
two fragments within him, hungry and destructive, one
feeding on the other. He was glad it was still dark.

He staggered and sobbed for a while, and then found
the train and took it back to Chicago. The car smelled of
cigarette smoke, and at this hour there was only one
other passenger, a black man wearing a baseball hat and
carrying a satchel. Before they got to the Loop, Parker
changed his seat – sat across the aisle from the man, and
turned his face to him, glared at him, imploring him,

daring the man to hurt him. But the man sniffed and muttered and went to the front of the car, leaving Parker feeling crazy and useless. He felt he could attract violence, but that man was decent, incapable of doing him harm. He went to Union Station. It was open, it was lighted.

He sat upright on a wooden bench that was like a church pew and he had, he knew, a sort of screwball's alertness: staring, wideawake, for no reason at all, at the posters in the ticket lobby. He examined each one with a critical eye, hating the fraudulent happiness in them – the happy couple in swimsuits, wetted by high sudsy surf, selling cigarettes. Look closely and you saw that each one had a cigarette, the man in his mouth, the woman in her fingers. Another ad demonstrated that explorers in distant jungles smoked Camels, and yet others proved that frenzied children drank Coke, that vodka drinkers got laid, that wise people read *Time*, that women with split skirts who had long beautiful legs wore Polly Panti-Hose and looked wickedly energetic, and as slender and healthy as the full-lipped woman lighting up a Virginia Slim. It was not the crude manipulation in the posters but rather their exuberance – and their foolish innocence – that drove him from the station while it was still night.

But even the darkest streets did not frighten him. Walking through shadows, under scaffolding, down narrow alleys, past blind doorways, he closed in on strangers as though challenging them to beat him down and rob him. He would not fight back. It excited him to know that he had only a few dollars and Ewa's police badge. His indifference gave him an unexpected strength – he wasn't afraid and he wasn't tired, and yet this day had been going on for days. No one approached him. He knew that he was nothing and that he was doomed. He could not make himself suffer. He felt only a horrible exaltation, and when he saw a cluster of filthy pigeons under the El at the edge of the Loop he menaced them. They flew up, squirting gobs of white shit as they clapped their stiff wings, and as they beat around his head, still shitting, it seemed a perfect image for the way he felt.

He returned to Union Station just after dawn to make the phone call he had been rehearsing all night.

'We've got to talk,' he said. 'I'll be right over.'

Ewa had been waiting for him just inside the main door downstairs, by the twelve doorbells. Seeing him, she stepped out and met him on the stairs. She did not stop but kept descending, past the milkbottles, to the broken bottom step, to the sidewalk.

Her military sunglasses hid her eyes, and he knew she probably hadn't slept either. She wore a light jacket, a tee-shirt under it, a pair of tough blue jeans rubbed pale at the knees, and her usual track shoes. It was what she had always worn. Why hadn't he guessed that she was a cop and that this was the plainclothes cop's uniform?

She said nothing, she was walking.

It was a bright Chicago morning – elderly brick buildings looking grey and low under the great dome of pale blue sky, and the air like thin heated gas. There was a twanging of traffic from the Stevenson Expressway at the end of the street, but no cars this early on Cottage Grove and no one up except a man tugging a small snuffling dog. The trash barrels were out. The trash had been collected earlier and they stood empty, the random clusters, looking fragile. Some litter remained, crumpled paper, smeared cans, blackened garbage. In this mess were the moving figures of pigeons pecking at crumbs, creeping ratlike through the litter. They were the same slow top-heavy birds that Parker had seen flapping and squirting under the El at the Loop. They looked filthy, too, but also quaint and senile, and a bit baffled, as though facing extinction.

'Can't we go back upstairs?' Parker said. How could he ask her for his wallet here?

But Ewa was still walking.

'I don't want you in there,' she said. She hadn't turned – she was headed north, towards the pigeons – and there were more pigeons and barrels further on. 'You're out of my life.'

Parker caught up with her and pleadingly said, 'You could have told me you were a cop.'

Touching his pocket, he seemed to indicate where the wallet was, and she reached over and easily retrieved it – batting his hand away and digging it out. She looked at the badge, she worked her thumb across the leather flaps, then she stuffed it into the pocket of her jacket and snorted.

'And you could have told me a few things,' Ewa said. 'Why is it that when people first meet they always try to act better than they are? They don't know each other, and so they lie. I didn't bullshit you, but you were all lies.'

'I had to – I loved you.'

'You didn't even know me – you're lying now! See what I mean?'

It was true, and it proved the truth of her accusation.

He said, 'I needed you – for a friend.'

'I don't want bullshitters for friends,' she said. 'I should break your fucking hands.'

She swept aside to face him, and planted her feet, and struck a fighting posture. Parker prepared himself to be hit: he held his breath and squinted. But there was sadness in her defiance, the way she dropped her hands after a few moments. Parker felt that at any second she might scream at him or burst into tears.

'Go away,' she said. 'Get back – I don't need you.'

It was not the violence in her voice but the simple

rejection in the words that hurt him. With Ewa the world made sense, and her presence had given him the hope that he might be able to bear his remorse. But losing her this way, as she fled down the street, meant losing the strength and the logic in her that he had come to depend on.

'Why didn't you tell me,' he said, 'that you're a cop?'

'I'm asking myself why you're so interested,' Ewa said. 'It's a lousy job. When you tell people about it they make stupid jokes, or they ask the wrong questions, or they run away. Hey, why didn't you tell me you were an asshole?'

'I'm worse than that,' he said, but she was moving fast, still striding. He felt heavy and fatigued. 'Ewa —'

That slowed her down, but only to pause and say, 'I hate hearing you say my name.' Then she was facing him. 'That's why I don't want you around. If I had to see you near me I'd start hating myself.'

'You're right,' he said. 'I know you're better off without me.'

She seemed surprised by the way he had agreed so quickly, but she recovered and walked on, more furious for his having surprised her.

'What's this?' she said, and flung something down, and kept walking. 'What's this?'

The lazy pigeons didn't fly, they just hopped and hobbled aside as Ewa scattered small white cards, clawing them from Parker's wallet. She left him stooping to scrape them from the sidewalk with his fingers as she strode ahead.

His Evanston Yacht Club card, his Delta Frequent Flyer, his credit cards – eight of them, and Shell and Esso charge cards; several of his boasting business cards, and one of Barbara's, and a portrait of her sealed in plastic and a snapshot of Eddie with his birthdate on the back; his Blackhawk Club key, and more . . .

'What's this? What's that?'

She was still flinging them down, and she did it expertly like snapping playing cards into a hat. There was violence in the motions of her arms and she was walking with such determination that Parker could barely keep up with her.

'And this, and this!'

It was money, about three hundred dollars in twenties and tens that he crumpled in his hands as he gathered it. And then she turned, because he was on his knees scrabbling among the pigeons which pecked at the money with their blunt smeared beaks.

'Who the hell are you?'

Her voice was so hard he wanted to cry. It was a real question and he had no answer.

The pigeons wobbled and extended their wings and prepared to fly off as Ewa emptied what remained in Parker's wallet beside an empty barrel. She then tossed the flimsy wallet to the ground.

'You're still married, you've got a kid, you live in Evanston, you're in about twenty clubs, your credit's great, you've got money – you're made –'

But Parker was still kneeling, scraping up cards and money, denying what she said and pleading with her to stop – for her sake, so that he could tell her that he was nothing, that he had wrecked himself and walked out of that life; that he was no one. And yet, even now, he knew he must not tell her he was a murderer. He did not want to be taken to jail, and locked up, and fed three times a day. Jail was suspense – no more. It wasn't punishment. He wanted something much worse than that.

'I trusted you,' Ewa was saying, in a voice that ached with her having been betrayed. But she did not sound as brokenhearted as she did vindictive. Parker knew that if she wished she could flatten him – choke him, kill him, break his bones, drive the wedgebone of his nose into his brain with the meat of her palm.

He wanted to say that he too had been betrayed: he had taken her for a lost soul, who needed him, who answered his Personal ad; and all the while she had been a cop. But that did not seem very important to him now; it was much worse that she was rejecting him, and he had never guessed that it would be so painful. He felt humiliated and desperate in a world that had become huge and inhospitable.

'Know what? I'd like to run you in,' Ewa said. 'I'd like to cuff you and haul your ass to the station and book you. I'd like to see you in the tank with your shoes off and a lot of druggies hitting on you. I'd love to see you in court, getting hammered.'

That seemed so civilized to Parker. He began to smile at the absurdity of it: it was a mark of how little she knew that she was offering him so little in the way of punishment – she was simply angry and hurt. She wasn't outraged, and she should have been. It was his fault that she wasn't. But he could not expect anything more from her. Once, he had never been able to decide whether she was a friend or a lover or one of his victims, but now he knew, and it frightened and appalled him. He stood shakily, hobbling to one side like a pigeon, and then stumbled and ran.

'Keep running, asshole,' Ewa said, in a deadly hiss as he passed her.

The pigeons flew off from under his feet, they fluttered, they beat their wings loudly and took away his last scrap of hope.

Then he had no one – no one to serve, no one to help him, no one to punish him properly; no one wanted him. He was dangerous, and he was solely responsible. There was no one else to blame or involve.

That morning he slept in Grant Park. He woke up sore, and yet surprised and sad that he was still alive. But it was a sick vitality rioting in him, a demoralizing confusion in his body that was not life but panic. There was only one place he could think of to go.

13

THE heatwave broke, and on the days that followed the sky was stacked with thunderheads, clouds like black mountains, which made everything around Chicago – the flat bright plains – look dramatic for once. Parker stood at the window of the room he had rented and he watched the silver vitreous rain crackling in the street.

He thought he had done a timid necessary thing, moving into a furnished room on South Blue Island Avenue. But it was as though he had jumped into a fast-flowing river and was being rushed along in its current. He was dressed as a woman now – that was the reason for his being driven down.

His room overlooked a cut-price liquor store, and beyond that, along the block, was a clothing store, a mattress discounter, and a grocer's, all of them with black steel grilles covering their plate-glass windows. The protective grilles made them look uncommercial and even forbidding, like supply depots under siege. This neighbourhood, known as The Island, was terrifying in its clutter and its graffiti and its loitering men; and it was noisy with all its hidden, contending radios. Yet Parker had not been harmed, and he was so casually threatened – people murmured and muttered, they swore but they didn't shout – he stopped worrying. The

Island was only terrifying for those who didn't live there.

He had been carried downstream. He slept alone and wished his old life away, that whole failure. He had known passion and sexual desire, and in between those spasms he had had glimpses of love. But love had not been enough: he was too damaged to hold it for long. He now looked back and saw how he had been cruel and unstable, how he had teased women with his personal ads and those lying letters he had written; how he had wrecked his feelings. He had been left with ruins – nothing to build on. So: dismantle those ruins. There was nothing that he could convert into friendship. Let it all drop into the dark.

He preferred the dark. He avoided daylight. He only went out at night – cruising, another watery word that suited the narrowing river he was submerged in. At first he tested himself in the clothes he had bought. He learned to walk in high heels. He entered bars and mingled with people – but at night it was nearly always men. There was no intimacy in any of this: he was a horror, half-alive, with hollow sooty eyes, lonely among women and even lonelier among men.

Strange men spoke to him all the time. Did this happen to all women at night? Men never talked to strange men, but as the solitary strange woman he was these nights, he was constantly greeted, heckled or subjected to obscene remarks. Drunks were the worst, the clumsiest, the most persistent. Most of the men were black down here. Were they attracted by his glossy wig? But he had to be blonde like Sharon. It could have been his tottering posture; the high heels forced him to stand upright with his chin out and his shoulders straight and, unsteady, he felt exposed. His dresses made him feel vulnerable too. He felt big and naked because of his light clothes, and he could not bring himself to reply to the men. He said nothing. He lowered his eyes and submitted.

Those were glancing encounters while he was still experimenting with the clothes – a chance remark in a bar, a snarl from a man passing in the street, the catcalls of boys sitting on front steps and hanging on playground fences. He disliked the remarks – they were all the same remark, really, vulgar echoes – but in dressing this way, looking outlandish and vulnerable, like a puppet, he had asked for it. It was the only way he could make sense of his life in this world. He found he was less sorrowful this way. It did not diminish his sense of remorse, but it clarified it and it contained that corrosive feeling.

And he didn't take the men's obscenities personally. Most men spoke to women as though they were transvestites: men too feeble and pathetic to wear men's clothes.

He had made his body hairless: that too made him feel physically weak. He used heavy make-up. He perfumed himself with cheap stuff. He looked comic, he knew; he smelled like disinfectant. But he could only bear himself this way. It was a necessity and a penance, but it was also a disguise, and that was a great relief.

He had a secret that no one must know: he was a murderer. With his teeth and his hands he had killed that poor girl Sharon in her depressing room. He had taken what little life she had away. He was worse than the Wolfman the newspapers had named. He had to be alone, to devise his own unique punishment. He had to be isolated and silent. Just by divulging his crime he would be doing harm.

Unexpectedly, the newspapers began mentioning 'Wolfman' again – another hunt for the killer, after a young woman was found murdered in her apartment on West Walton. She had been picked up at a nearby singles bar and strangled soon afterwards. There were teethmarks on the body. There had been a time when Parker had longed to see such a news item as this, that would prove that he was not the killer, because he had not committed this crime. But now he knew better. He had seen Sharon's grave. He had probably inspired this West Walton murder.

The singles bar was called 'Sweethearts'. The innocent name was printed on tee-shirts and coffee cups that were for sale at the entrance. Parker was discouraged by the silly souvenirs and by the joky tone of the bar – the stuffed toys on the wall with the varsity pennants. He wanted something vicious – darker and more dangerous than this place. The men inside were sightseers and tourists, definitely from out of town – they were overdressed, they wore hats. The only Chicagoans there had probably come out of curiosity, because of the murder. That was Parker's reason too, but he reminded himself that unlike those other men he was not a spectator: he was not a man.

The summer rain was a help to him; he wore a raincoat over his black dress and felt less obvious and misshapen. He chose to sit alone in a booth and he kept his coat on. He was glad for the bad light and the shadows. The music was very loud but that distraction was also an advantage. He had been hoping to avoid the sort of bright quiet bar where he would easily be seen as a freak.

The deceitfulness of what he was doing here in this public place, dressed as a woman, struck him as almost criminal, and when he heard a clear voice rise from the murmurs and say – *like that dyke over there*, he believed that he was meant.

A waitress wearing a 'Sweethearts' tee-shirt put a tray down on Parker's table and placed a glass of beer in front of him.

'A guy at the bar bought it for you,' the waitress said.

The heart motif on the tee-shirt was shaped around one of her breasts. Parker was in awe of the simplicity of her body, her trusting face. She was young and at first she made him feel like a clown, and then he saw that it was his remorse that made him altogether different from her. He felt awkward and overdressed. He was disguised, yes, but his disguise was self-defeating, since it made him so conspicuous.

But who had bought him this drink? No one whom he could see – and yet he was touched by the gesture, the kindness in it, someone seeing him. Or was it more than that – someone recognizing him?

'Hi. Mind if I join you?'

Parker looked up and saw the man hovering, and he was startled by the man's bulk. He was heavy, with glasses clamped crookedly on his pink nose. He had a short thick neck, he was in his fifties probably, and not shiny bald but with irregular patches on his scalp where his hair was missing – it looked rubbed away. What hair he had was too long and needed a trim, and his hairy ears seemed too small for his head.

'Please – have a seat,' Parker said softly.

The man stared at the sound of Parker's voice, looking towards his lips. His glasses slightly distorted his eyes, and his jacket was soaked on the shoulders; probably he had been walking around in the rain trying to work up the courage to come into this bar.

'I got that for you,' he said, gesturing to the glass of beer in front of Parker. And he had brought his drink with him. He wagged it in his hand, rattling the cubes, and he sipped it noisily. The man's nervousness made him seem ugly and slow-witted, but Parker felt sorry for him. How threatening the man seemed, and Parker knew that the man was unaware of this apparent menace and was simply a blunderer.

The man's fear made Parker calm. In that same soft voice, Parker said, 'What's your name?'

This seemed to rouse the man and put him on guard. He squirmed and said, 'Never mind.'

'You're not from Chicago, are you?'

'Gary – well, near enough, Hobart.' But saying this the man winced and the pain stayed in his eyes, as though he regretted having told the truth. 'What's with all the questions? I mean, who wants to know?'

Parker lifted his glass and drank, and the man looked away, as though trying to decide what to do next.

'I've never been in here before,' Parker said, and so the man would not take it as a criticism he added, 'But it's very nice – very lively. It's young, though.'

The man said, 'How about another drink?'

'No thanks.'

'Let's go then,' the man said, and went outside hurriedly.

On the sidewalk, Parker said, 'Are you surprised I agreed so quickly?'

'I thought that was the whole idea,' the man said. 'Let's go – my hotel's a few blocks over.'

'I can't go there,' Parker said. 'They watch the hotels – there are police, you know.'

'What are you saying?'

'You could come to my place.'

The man said, 'I ain't falling for that one' and began looking away. He wanted to leave but he did not know how to begin. Finally he said, 'Excuse me. I've got to go find a john. I'll be right back.'

The man did not return of course – Parker knew he wouldn't. Parker drifted down the street and then walked away. It had only been an experiment, and it had worked, because he had believed in himself. He was Sharon. He had not failed; the man had. And yet, that he was able so easily to slip into this disguise and this life and become Sharon – this proved to him that he was dangerous and tricky.

He felt that – the deceit – again the next day, lying in his small hot room, with the shades drawn and little seams of brightness where the sunlight broke through the worn fabric of the shade. He was waiting for the day to grow dark so that he could stir.

He set off again that night, walking up Blue Island Avenue and assuming he would be accosted. Some men muttered 'Blondie' as he passed, but he was not threatened.

He came to attention when a woman approached him and began speaking. She was black, with a hairnet, wearing jeans and sneakers and a radio station tee-shirt.

'Know where there's a pay-phone around here, honey?'

'Just back there,' Parker said, because he remembered passing one with youngsters in the booth and hanging around it. 'But be careful.'

'Don't worry about me,' the woman said, and touched his arm.

The confident way she touched him moved him enormously: it was the first human contact he had had in weeks, and it made him hesitate in his resolve. He considered going after the woman, he wished he had her as a friend – or someone like her. But no, he didn't deserve her. If she had known who he was – a man, a murderer disguised as his victim – she would never have gone near him.

Nearer the university a group of men – four or five, it was dark and he didn't look back – burst out of a side street and followed him. When Parker walked faster they did the same, and they edged closer and spoke to him.

'Hey, slow down – don't run away.'

'Leave her alone, Angie. She sucks.'

'Here, you want some of this? Hey, chicky, ever seen one of these before?'

'Come on with us – we want to open your hole. You'd like that, eh?'

Just as though they knew he was a man and was taunting him because of his clothes.

'Come over here, I want to show you something.'

He wanted to go. But he knew men. They didn't mean any of this – it was bravado, nothing more. They would humiliate him a little and show off and then they'd leave him. In this bullying strutting group they were practically harmless. It was only alone that they would be as savage as they pleased.

'She's smiling – she likes it.'

They kept this up and then, when Parker did not respond – kept walking, said nothing – they dropped away and laughed and he looked back. After a block and a half one of the men detached himself from the group and followed him. The man pretended to be calm and unhurried, but he moved quickly towards Parker, determined to catch up.

'Hold on,' the man said.

Parker looked at the man. Away from the others this one was quieter. He was about thirty, he wore a short-sleeved shirt, and by the neon lighting in the front window of a nearby bar the man's face, Parker decided, was Irish, that sort of chin and cheeks.

'You want a drink?'

Why was it that all men said that to women they hated but wanted? Perhaps there was something in their bitter desire that made them think of thirst.

'That would be lovely,' Parker said.

The man pretended not to be surprised; pretended, on the contrary, to have the advantage, because Parker had agreed so promptly.

The bar was gloomy and full of men, and Parker saw how the man distanced himself from Parker – didn't touch him. He was ashamed of him, ashamed of himself. Something in that shame suggested to Parker that the man was violent.

He breathed in Parker's face when he spoke to him. 'You were waiting for me, right?'

Parker said nothing. He was self-conscious about his deep voice. He was more confident in a bar like this, though – glad for the smoke and the noise and the darkness; glad for the indifference of the bad-tempered drinkers.

'What do you want?' the man said.

'Whatever you want,' Parker said.

'That's impossible.'

What had he said wrong?

The man glared at him and drew his lips back – sneering, hesitating, he might have been crazy. He had fleshy ears and freckles and a chin with a dent in it, and his forearms were burned. He was a labourer, he worked outside. He lowered his head. He did not speak directly to Parker.

'I want you on your knees. I want you begging to eat it.'

'Yes,' Parker said.

His eagerness disappointed the man.

'If you make me,' Parker said.

That was better, the man's ears registered pleasure. He whispered, 'I want to see another guy's cold come dripping out of your snatch.'

He had made himself breathless from uttering this sentence: he was eager and embarrassed. He wanted to say more, Parker could tell, but he did not know how to frame another incriminating statement. His gasping was enough: there was savagery in that foul air.

'Let's go to my place,' Parker said. 'It's not far.'

The man didn't say yes. He gulped his whisky and left hurriedly; and he was waiting a little distance from the bar when Parker walked outside. There was no other conversation. The strange sudden brutal things that men said to strange women – said only to women. It was all violent and hideous, but it was much more predictable than Parker had ever guessed. Men did not even make a pretence of talking any other way. Perhaps it was just talk, perhaps it was harmless?

The man kept his distance, following more like a dog than a human, and Parker knew that he was relieved that inside the room there was only the dim stripy light from the street; no lamps on. The man stumbled to the closet, opened doors, fumbled with the curtains, making sure they were alone. Parker heard the coarse scraping sound of the nervous man breathing through his nose.

'You're a hooker,' the man said. 'What are you, some nympho? You just go with anyone?'

The man hated himself and didn't know it. So he was almost certain to be violent.

'Yes,' Parker said. 'Anyone.'

'What do you do?'

'Anything that men want – everything.'

The man made a louder sound in his nose, but with that same scraping, showing that he was impressed. In a tremulous voice, he said, 'Tell me all about it. Get down and tell me.'

Parker dropped to his knees. He said, 'They tie me up. Some of them beat me.'

'You love it.'

Parker hesitated, then said, 'If you do.'

The man said, 'You're a sicko. You're a fucking screamer. Go on, I want to hear more.'

'Do whatever you want,' Parker said.

'Tell me about pain.'

'I get off on it. Give me some – now. I'm a pain freak. I'm an enema slave.'

At that moment, saying that and persuading himself that it was true, he had a vivid sight of the whipped genitals in the photograph by Robert Mapplethorpe, and he remembered Jakes saying *That's how life is – people do those things*, and remembered denying it. Now he thought *I am one of those people*, and he saw that the most savage photographs had been of him.

'I don't believe this,' the man said, as though speaking to another person in the room.

Parker reached for him, but when he was touched the man lashed out as though he had been bitten: 'Don't touch me!' he cried, and he kicked Parker very hard, catching him first in the chest and then in the face. Parker howled and fell over, clutching his face. He crouched there, expecting more. His ears rang and he could not tell whether the man was speaking, but after a few moments the voice was distinct.

'Did I hurt you?' The man seemed worried that this might be so, and he was now more like a boy than a man.

'No,' Parker said.

He wanted worse than that, worse than this impotent and fearful Irish voyeur; and yet he was also terrified. He wanted it to be sudden and violent and final. He had not expected this much meaningless humiliation and useless pain – or this much talk. But the man needed the talk: he was ineffectual and could not take it further.

'What are you doing?' Parker said. 'What do you want?'

The man was fumbling against the wall, probably looking for a lightswitch or a doorknob.

'Getting out of here,' the man said. 'You're sick.'

When the man was gone and his footsteps vanished on

the stairs, Parker began to cry. Not for what the man had done to him, but for the man's fear and panic, and for what he had done to that man.

14

THERE was something about the Chicago heat
rising from the filthy bricks of these ugly buildings
that gave a peculiar piercing clarity to men's voices, even
when they were mingled with street noise. And they
always said the same thing in different words.

'Hey, get over here, baby,' they said. 'I want to tell
you something –'

As though they knew this sad woman with the humid
hanging-down hair, so tentative in her new shoes.

'Here, you want a ride?' they said. 'You want a drink?
You want some barbecue.'

They are not questions, they are demands.

'What are you doing down here?' one man said. He
was black, with a huge mouth that looked as though it
was made of iron, and a jaw that was hinged and hard
like a wrench. He looked hungry and dangerous. His
teeth took hold of the same words again and insisted,
'What are you doing down here?'

It was the hardest question Parker had ever been asked.
He went silent and fled from the man, because the answer
was unbearable.

Most men's voices were like their hands – tough, thick,
casual, familiar, intrusive. You wanted them to stop,
because they didn't know what they were doing or
saying. Men touched him all the time. You only had to

go near a man for him to put his fingers on you, snatch at your clothes or flick you with his fingers. Some of them held his arm and looked him over when he paused, and they were probably surprised by the muscle underneath that blouse.

There were usually three or four standing together, and sometimes one on his own hissed at him, said 'Come here' or muttered 'bitch'.

He wanted them, but because of the very way they murmured these demands, their inhibiting familiarity made it impossible. How could they mean it when, standing in a group, they called him over? And what then? They would be deeply embarrassed if he went back and said, 'Okay – what do you want?'

Men were humiliated if you gave them what they asked for. Instead – you had to give them what they wanted, which was to humiliate you: to talk, to pinch, to swear, to spit and say the vilest words. But nothing beyond that. It was a little ritual of mortification – to go this far but no further. Now and then he saw a woman respond to these hollow taunts, but she didn't know she was making it awkward for the men. Parker knew: he had been a man.

It was no use to him that men needed to talk when they couldn't act: that words were enough for them, sometimes blunt shocking words. These days, as Sharon, he had found himself going to the Loop to stare at the heights of the Sears Tower and the clouds whipped past it, giving it motion, like a skyscraper on the march. One day, on the Rapid Transit between Halstead and Clinton, a man in a dark blue pin-striped suit, wearing a silk tie and a blue button-down shirt – a man about forty-five, no more, healthy face, carefully combed light hair, brown eyes, a slight scar on his chin, carrying a briefcase, too successful-looking for this particular stop – not a college professor, more like a broker giving someone on the Finance Committee some sound investment advice – this man walking quickly through the car, looked straight into Parker's eyes and frowned and said to him, 'Suck a cock.'

The whole encounter had taken four seconds, no more; but it had gouged his memory.

He needed that man, all those men, and yet their violence was not enough. They wanted to humiliate him when what he desired was to be destroyed.

You had to know that when they called out, 'Come here,' they meant *Go away*. Parker knew their pride, that they were preoccupied by their own pleasure and fear. But because of his helpless need for them, that they teased and yet would not answer, Parker looked for the company of women. Women pitied him and saw him as a freak, but they asked no questions.

He left his room. The Sears Tower in the Loop was the limit of his travel, the very edge of his world, and it was now like a monument to him. One afternoon he was returning from the Sears Tower to his building and at the junction of the West 15th and South Blue Island a car came to a sudden stop near him, braking at such speed that it swerved and mounted the kerb and scraped a newspaper-vending machine.

A man in sunglasses got out quickly and stumbled in anger to the passenger side, saying, 'If that's what you want –'

Parker simply stared at this chaotic scene.

The new Taurus was tilted on the kerb as the man dragged a women from the front seat – she wore a bright blue jersey and pale cream slacks and she raised her hands to protect her face. The man was furious, he pushed her away from the car, but didn't hit her.

He said loudly, 'You can stay here, then!'

162

The woman recoiled and began to cry, and the man made a gesture with his hands meaning that he was now rid of her. He reversed the car and drove away fast, heading east towards the expressway.

Parker watched the woman, wondering what she would do. At first he thought she might cry some more, but no – she seemed to relax, she blew her nose and took a deep breath. And from the way she looked around, from just the movement of her head, Parker felt certain that the woman was here for the first time, on what she regarded as one of the most dangerous streets in Chicago.

Parker suspected, without knowing why, that this abandoned woman represented hope for him. This suspicion strengthened his confidence, because he knew he would have to approach her and make a friend of her and help her, and then he would have his answer. No one else had seen the way she had been flung out of the car. Perhaps that was it: as a witness he felt he had a responsibility, and that he would be rewarded for it.

The woman was about forty, and darkish – Italian or Greek, although you never knew, she might be Peruvian, or Turkish or Arab. From the way she was dressed, in those casual clothes, so bright and clean, and with her hair done and cheap chunky jewellery – a matching bracelet and necklace set with stones that looked like Christmas candy – she looked as though she were dressed for a long journey.

Before Parker could say anything the woman drew her mouth down and said in a knowing nasal way, 'Am I wearing something of yours?'

Parker was terrified, and found himself answering her, saying no, before he realized that the woman was abusing him. Then he said, 'I just wanted to say that I saw what happened.'

'Where am I?' the woman said. 'We were going to the Dan Ryan.'

The woman's voice became even sharper, almost fierce. Was it because she was frightened? She was hardly safe here, alone on the South Side, having just been ejected from a car, which had driven off. She showed no interest in the passing cars, had not even turned to see where the Taurus had gone.

'Maybe he'll come back,' Parker said, wondering why the woman hadn't looked.

'I couldn't care less,' the woman said. It was not possible for anyone to say this sentence with total conviction, and yet this woman almost succeeded. She wore particularly lurid mascara, blackish-silver, that gave her lids the glitter of fish-scales. 'And I won't be here if he does.'

'Want a coffee?' Parker said.

The woman looked around and said, 'We're the only white people here.'

Parker was going to say *I hadn't noticed*, which was what he felt, but he knew the woman would not believe him.

'You're going to wreck your feet in those shoes,' the woman said. 'You're looking at someone who destroyed her feet that way. Yeah, I'd love a coffee.'

Parker touched his wig. He was always afraid at a moment like this that it might slip and betray him. The woman's lack of suspicion reminded him that she was looking at a woman and not a man – and Parker was a white woman who probably seemed more pathetic than she was. Actually she didn't seem pathetic at all, only uncomfortable in her tight clothes and hot sticky make-up.

'It's down here,' Parker said. It was only when the woman began walking that Parker saw her clumsiness, her heavy arms and thighs hindering her and moving her sideways.

The woman was too breathless from the walking to

say anything, but when after two blocks they arrived at Parker's building she said, 'I thought we were going to a coffee shop.'

She hesitated, frowned at the building, and now Parker saw the place with her eyes – the scarred door, the graffiti, the litter, the discs of chewing gum hardened on the steps, the pigeon shit, the battered grilles on the windows.

'It's not as bad as it looks,' Parker said, because he knew what the woman was thinking. 'I moved here not too long ago.'

And he had not stopped believing that this woman, whose plight he alone had witnessed and whom he had rescued from the street, would reveal something to him, and perhaps save him.

'Rick was always threatening to do something like that,' the woman said, mounting the stairs heavily, seeming to take possession of the building as she stamped each stair with her foot. She was speaking almost with admiration, panting between each phrase, at the way she had been thrown out of the car. 'Then he goes and does it. I didn't think he would.'

'Is he your husband?' Parker said.

'Does it make a difference?' the woman said, in that fierce tone again. 'Like, is it worse if you happen to be married to the guy that beats up on you?'

She seemed to be scolding him again – it was the same tone as *Am I wearing something of yours?* Obediently, Parker opened the door to his room. He had become keenly aware of the stink on the landing, and the sight of all the padlocked doors, and the bare bulbs hanging from the tin ceiling.

'Luxury,' the woman said. 'You paint it yourself? It's hotter in here than it is outside. Like, where do you sit?'

She walked past the small sofa not seeming to realize

that it was a sofa. She went to the window, twitched the curtains, looked into the street – there was always someone and usually two or three people standing in the street here – and then she glanced back into the room, made a sour face, and worked her fingertips together as though everything she touched was dusty.

Parker held up a jar. 'It's just instant, I'm afraid.'

'I'm not fussy.' A lie: there was fussiness in the way she said it.

There was no kitchen, there was a sink in the corner and a table next to it, and a scorched microwave and an electric kettle on the table.

The woman was silent – thinking. Parker had the idea that the enormity of what had happened to her had just struck her – that she had been thrown overboard by that angry man, flung from the car which had sped away.

Parker said, 'Don't worry.'

'I'm not worried.'

That meant she was, the way she replied, snapping at him.

'You'll be all right.'

She looked at Parker as though he was very small.

'I've been in worse places,' she said. 'Any Sweet and Low? I'm not allowed to have sugar.'

Parker shook his head, he had nothing like that, and the woman looked discouraged and weary when she was handed the cup.

'I'm Sharon,' Parker said.

'Vickie,' the woman said, and looked around and made no move to sit down. She sniffed and squinted. She said, 'There's something about this place. I don't know.'

'It's all I could afford,' Parker said.

'I don't mean that. It's probably lovely for this part of Chicago. It's something else.'

'Is it the light?'

'I just got through saying I don't know.'

And her mascara glittered, black and silver, as she challenged him with her face. Her lips were fat and shapeless.

'If I thought it was the light I would have said so.'

Parker said, 'You're probably wondering where the bed is.'

'I wasn't wondering,' the woman said.

'That little sofa,' Parker said. 'It's just six styrofoam cubes covered with cloth. You rearrange them, put them side by side and it becomes a bed.'

Without taking her eyes off him, the woman edged away, becoming wary and roundshouldered, as though in self-defence.

'I woke up this morning thinking I needed a woman friend,' Parker said. 'Then I went out. I don't know what made me. Then I saw you get thrown out of the car.'

Hearing this, the woman looked at Parker with distaste.

'I was glad to get away from that bozo,' the woman said.

This wasn't true at all. Parker had seen her crying.

'I went willingly.' And she laughed, like three pushes on a pump.

The woman was lying, but why, after what she had been through? Instead of seeing what had happened as extraordinary she was content to regard it as conventional, as though every day women were being pushed out of cars on the South Side by angry men who drove off and didn't come back.

This woman Vickie was strong and selfish – was that what he had had to learn? Or had he been wrong? Since finding her on the street, almost since the first words she had spoken, Parker had disliked her. She was objectionable; he could not imagine her as a friend. By degrees, in the room, he had lost interest in her. Parker now wanted to know more about the man who had thrown her out of the car, and in the presence of Vickie he began to see that man as emotionally bruised and tormented – he had suffered.

Silenced by these thoughts, Parker had drifted to the window to watch the boys playing noisily in the street. The woman had not said anything since her last lie, and yet Parker knew she was staring at him – he felt her attention, the weight of it against the back of his neck.

Finally, she said, 'So what do you do, take it off at night?'

She was looking with sour scrutiny at his hair.

'What do you mean?' Parker said.

The woman's gaze tightened on him as she stepped back in fear.

'Stay where you are,' she said. She was at the door. 'You put a finger on me and I'll scream.' She opened the door. She said, 'You've got some nerve, mister.'

'I couldn't hurt you,' Parker said. 'I've already murdered someone. It was terrible.'

It was the plain truth, but his words were like black flames, driving the woman out of the door and down the stairs, and he saw her in the street, not looking back at his building.

The room seemed much emptier then, Parker himself diminished by the woman's departure. But he had needed to tell her what he had done, and he had wanted her to leave.

It was always a mistake for him to go out in daylight. He belonged to the dark.

Mapplethorpe's exhibition was still on at the Museum of Contemporary Art, 'Mapplethorpe' still huge on the banner hanging limply in the heat from the front of the building. Out of curiosity, and because he had nothing else to do, Parker returned to the exhibition and saw the men in leather and the nudes and the slave collars and the bloody genitals and the swollen flesh, and it seemed to him now that the photographs had a dignity and a directness that he had not seen before. They had pathos, they had humour, they did not seem freakish; some seemed to Parker tragic. But praising the photograph of a man who was startlingly sick – the last picture in the show – Parker attracted the attention of a bearded man, who turned to him and said, 'It's very sad, isn't it? He's got it.'

The photograph by Jakes showed his friend looking cadaverous, with sunken cheeks and hollow eyes – his whole small skull obvious in his face. He seemed like a marooned man, someone who had been left on a desert island for many years, just scratching and clawing for food, growing thinner, with wasted muscle and fragile skin; it was the face of a man lost and doomed.

It was a month old, and had been taken not long after Parker and Barbara had seen the show. In that time Mapplethorpe had fallen ill, and he had apparently summoned Jakes, who had taken his self-portrait, and added it to the others. *He's got it*, meant only one thing, and Parker who had hated him now grieved for him.

That same day, as it was growing dark, Parker took the train to Skokie and went to Sharon's grave. He brought flowers, he arranged them in front of the stone which now had Sharon's name carved on it. He knelt and tried to pray, but his words were no more than futile protests – he was whining. And it did no good. Sharon wasn't there.

He had thought that taking on Sharon's identity might eventually rid him of his remorse. He was no less remorseful, but he began to know Sharon better. She was twitchy and reckless – tearful, needy, frustrated, impulsive, dangerous at times. She had done no harm, but how was it possible that someone so innocent could be so lonely? Yet it was so. Innocence didn't strengthen you, it made you solitary and lonelier; it placed you at risk. And loneliness diminished Parker so completely that most of the time he felt invisible, as Sharon must have.

These days he seldom spoke to anyone except to ask for something at a store – the cans of food that he warmed up in the little microwave which had come with the room, or the take-away meals he bought from the fearful, agitated Vietnamese man at the end of his block: greasy noodles, wet vegetables. When someone, even that skinny man, spoke the simplest formula of greeting or farewell, 'How are you doing?' or 'Have a good one,' something in Parker's heart was stirred, and he felt foolishly grateful. Afterwards, he was more lonely for what he knew he was missing.

He bought a cheap black-and-white television set that was no bigger than his microwave and in most ways resembled it. He left this television on all day, and it flickered until he went to bed. Always lighted and chattering importantly, it gave the room a semblance of life. He often listened to his radio at the same time, and it consoled him to be at the centre of the ragged, contending noise.

His interest was now directed to public events. He was drawn to the news, to murders and disappearances and scandals, to announcements about poisoned aspirin, or revelations of a jailed singer, to the latest drug craze or the disclosures of teenage heroin users whose pregnancies resulted in addicted infants. Sharon had followed those stories – all lonely people did. Lonely people lose sleep over the Ayatollah and the Ozone Layer.

Great and small, the presidential campaign, the forest

fires in Yellowstone, the drought in the midwest, medical waste – used syringes and bloody bandages – polluted beaches in New York, the disappearance of a little girl in a well in Texas, the car crash of a familiar newscaster, the death of a whale on a remote beach in California, a spate of muggings, the hijacking of airliners – disaster, tragedy, terrorism – he followed each story, and he knew that all over the country other lonely people were doing the same.

The details were repeated from hour to hour, sometimes with slight variations, sometimes with new developments, until they seemed to displace the events in Parker's own life, overwhelming his memory of the murder he had committed, and often abstracting him from his feelings of remorse, as he waited for statements, more details, further reports. This news consumption was like his desperate appetite for junk food, and in just the same way it deepened his hunger, for junk drinks had always made him thirstier, and hamburgers increased his capacity to eat more; and bad news made him need worse news.

It had become so that only the tragedies attracted him – the unhappy faces, the bodies being blow-torched from train wrecks, the eyewitness accounts of fires in Korean hotels, of people made homeless through the implacable dynamitings of Israeli soldiers, and shattered corpses and luggage strewn across a field amid the wreckage of a crashed plane. He watched closely as eyewitnesses tried to describe their shock, and he loathed himself for noticing how badly dressed survivors of tragedies always were.

He ate junk food and watched junk television, and he knew that Donohue and Geraldo were talking to him, just as he knew that the men on the radio talk-shows were addressing him. They were now more familiar to him than Ewa or Barbara had ever been. He slept a great deal, leaving either the television or the radio on, and when he was depressed or when the man on the news team said, '*I'm following that airliner story, Jack, and I'll give you a live update at five,*' he watched game shows, and he became involved in the lives of the contestants.

'*Jay, you're a computer programmer in Anaheim and your wife Dale works in a flower shop designing floral bouquets, and you have two boys, and your hobby is collecting railway memorabilia, and your ambition is to visit London and Paris.*'

How complete people's lives seemed.

'*Well, we know your kids are eight and ten, and we have a whole host of wonderful prizes for you and them if you win. A wall of sound music system by Sony, with a CD player and the whole quadriphonic package. You'll love the Allbright Workmaster power tools, and your wife will step into a new fragrance with our prize of a range of cosmetics by Nina Ricci . . .*'

But Jay and Dale Ashby lost to the Nemhards from Minneapolis, and Parker became inexpressibly sad, until he saw in the next round that the Nemhards were worthier winners.

He watched 'Wheel of Fortune' and was maddened when a contestant could not guess, from the letters on the board, simple expressions such as *hostess with the mostest* or *my old Kentucky home*, and those were among the few times that Parker spoke, seeing the baffled face of the person after Vanna White turned the letter (*yes, we have one*) and chanting, 'On the road to Mandalay – On the road to Mandalay –'

He was reassured by the regularity of the programmes and the same talk, the same catch-phrases and quiz-masters, the same quartet on the news team. And he was sorry when Shelley, the weatherman, went on vacation, and even somewhat surprised that these people had another life outside television, for he had begun to be persuaded that television represented the whole of their existence, in the same way that his watching it represented the whole of his.

This was Sharon's life, these shows, the news, this room. It was not enough.

Parker bought the newspaper to follow the programmes and plan his day, and he kept them – and a new aversion to cleaning the room (it seemed to reduce it and make it seem depressingly bare) made him keep the papers and reread the classifieds. The *Tribune* bored him. These days he always bought the *Reader*.

The personal ads fascinated him and fed his imagination, and he could discern very clearly – from the wording alone, the way it was always coded – the crazy ones, the reckless ones, the marriage-minded ones, the slobs, the ones into pain or just taking a chance, the gays, the kinks, the couples, the first-timers, the bullies, the desperate ones, people who were simply, screamingly lonely.

All men – why was this? – used most of their ad space describing their ideal woman, which was not a woman at all, but a girl, always young, usually small, 'well-built': the absurdity of a busty little girl! – willing to try anything, preferably blonde; a bunny, a victim.

Women's ads never said those things, seldom described the man at all, but concentrated on the woman searching, as in *Woman, forty-something, relocating in the Chicago area, a nursing/physiotherapy background, interested in food, wine, music, books, nights out, travel, but sick of the singles scene* . . . No mention of wanting a man tall or short, young or old, thin or fat, though sometimes there was a mention of 'non-smoker'. Women advertised the facts of their lives; men described their fantasies.

Parker did not fit the description in any of these male fantasies, although he knew that in crucial ways he was perfect: Sharon, the victim, was a natural for personal ads. These men wanted fantasy sex, fantasy lives, fulfilled dreams of pleasure and success, the complete existence of

173

people on television programmes, the contestants on 'Family Feud' or 'Wheel of Fortune' or 'The Price is Right' – those wise-cracking couples who shrieked and clapped and said, 'All right!' and 'Go for it!' And some of the men who advertised in personal columns wanted to commit acts of mayhem and murder. All the ads suggested violence, but how could you be absolutely sure?

Lying in bed at night, with the stripes of headlights moving across the wall and rippling over him, Parker murmured, reciting and improving his ideal personal ad, which went, *Remorseful WF, 37, pretty, blonde, desperate, living alone, reasonably wealthy, own car, non-smoker, seeks man to execute her. Genuine offers only.*

But wasn't that the message of all personal ads, no matter whose?

He sometimes saw an ad that roused him and made him think that he had only to answer it for justice to be done and for him to be at peace. What struck him about such ads was that they were precisely the sort he had once put in the *Reader*, though livelier and more explicit. *Creative DWM into body-building and photography anxious to meet small submissive F 20–30, any race or nationality, to share fantasies. Total discretion assured. Photo please.*

And there were sometimes dream ads that promised humiliation, punishment, violence, but with a mention of pleasure or fun so perfunctory that it was like a promise of hurt.

Nearly always you had to write to a box number. Parker knew that routine well. But now and then there was a first name and a Chicago number.

'Hello?'

Parker was gagging, trying to reply, but his chest had tightened, and his voice, which he hardly used, was inaudible.

'I can't hear you. I don't –'

'It's about your ad in the *Reader*.'

'You sound pretty strange,' the voice said. 'Hey, what do you look like?'

'Not too tall,' Parker said. 'About average height –'

'You sound like a guy. Is this a guy? Listen, if this is a guy – hey, say something else.'

Parker quickly put the receiver down. There were two other numbers. One was constantly busy, the other elicited a reply in a voice that had a low gurgle of pure lunacy that made Parker speechless.

If he had had the time, he would have written a letter, enclosed a picture, and hoped to be savagely murdered by the first man he met. But he was nervous and impatient. He knew he deserved to die, but he wanted his death to be certain. He did not want to be hammered on the head and left a lingering humiliated cripple, unable to finish the job.

He missed – what? Not Barbara or the baby. Not his parents, not Ewa. All of them were well rid of him. He missed his childhood, something he could hardly remember, a still and solitary period, before he had entered the world, when time had seemed limitless and death had no meaning; when everything had seemed possible to him and he had had a strong sense of his superiority. Before he had known any pain, before he had known love; when he had lived in a mood of dumb grateful joy. Experiencing love he had begun to die, and physical love had weakened him. Sex was always destructive, and self-love led only one way – Sharon knew that.

Men had always called to her, 'Come here, come here.'

15

H E felt frail and yet indestructible, as though he
would always hold on, like an infection that recedes
but never clears. His old sense of being dangerous returned
to him and made him cautious: he saw how he had
provoked these men. What disturbed him most were the
reactions he excited in the men. He knew he was still
capable of doing harm. He had thought, dressed as a
woman, that he was condemned to be a victim. But it
was more complicated than that. As a woman – as *this*
woman – he began to understand Sharon's complicity,
her share of the violence. He saw the subtleties of justice,
that she was to blame for some of her suffering, but she
had not deserved to die. She had offered herself as a
submissive lover, to please him, and he had killed her for
it. Was death the natural consequence of such desire? Was
murder a bloody image for the briefest love affair?

These thoughts gave him more days of recrimination,
and at the end of them he had to force himself to go
out.

The rest was simple but alarming. All he had to do was
dress as a woman and leave the building and he was
swept along: it was something he had never experienced
as a man. He was borne along by men – their talk, their
stares, their very presence, as they surrounded and
crowded him and moved him on. He did not resist. He

kept walking. He was surprised by how far you could get on foot, in these shoes – he was almost to Roosevelt.

There, at a pay-phone that had a hood like a hairdryer, he called Barbara in Evanston. He mumbled into the receiver when Barbara said hello. He had not spoken aloud for almost a week, and his voice, almost a whisper, was strange to him, and to Barbara, too.

'Who is this?' Barbara said, her voice harsh and demanding. 'Parker, is that you?'

'I don't know what –' But the words softened and went dead.

'Is this something to do with my husband?'

Parker's voice was inaudible – the words stayed in his mouth.

'Listen, what have you done with my husband?'

'Still alive,' Parker said.

She hadn't heard. She was still talking. 'The police are looking for him. Now if you have any information –'

He hung up. It was hopeless. She was stridently alive, and that was all that mattered. It had been a mistake to call, it had only roused her: he had no news for her.

Before he had turned from the phone there was a man next to him, talking, the way they always did, as though to someone awful and small whom they knew from way back, big with bullying, the masculine voice bearing down, pressuring and insisting – because he was a woman, at night, alone.

It was so predictable. You could go into a bar. There were stares at first, a certain kind of temporary silence, and then someone would come over and begin to talk like that. A woman only had to show up and then she was taken the rest of the way, whether she wanted it or not.

The man wore a hat and was fattish, his shirt stretched tight over his paunch. He wasn't white, he wasn't black, he was something swarthy inbetween and looked grumpy and sounded short-tempered and impatient.

'Don't kid me, you're not going anywhere,' he said, because Parker had turned away from him. 'You're looking for me, aren't you?'

The man didn't wait for an answer. He took Parker's hand, holding it with big soft fingers, and he hailed a taxi.

'South Blue Island Avenue, at Throop,' Parker said to the driver.

The man jammed Parker's hand roughly between his thighs and said nothing.

In the room, he insisted on putting on a small light. He said disgustedly, 'No air-conditioner.' He removed his shirt and yawned, making a loud growling. His hair was short and stiff but it grew down the back of his neck and spread across his shoulders, like a covering of fur.

Parker, who had been watching from a low chair where he crouched forward, said, 'I just want to say something.'

'Go ahead,' the man said.

Parker said, 'Every Saturday a guy took a different girl to his fraternity house and when they left his room a few hours later the guys watching knew that he had screwed her – she had that dazed and spaced-out look. Just to find out how he managed to have such success with women they put a mike in his room and tape-recorded what went on –'

He hesitated. The man was peering at him, but Parker could not make out the expression on his face.

'Afterwards, they listened to the tape,' Parker said. 'All they heard were the sounds of the woman being beaten up.'

'Is that supposed to be funny?' the man said.

'It was why the guy was so successful with women,' Parker said. 'Because he slapped them around.'

178

The man grunted and glanced behind him, spooked by Parker's whispered story. Then he seized Parker's arm and dragged him to a kneeling position. He was in a hurry, he was aroused.

'You know what to do with it,' he said.

Parker didn't have the slightest idea, and ignorant terror made him clumsy. He hated kneeling before this man, yet he also knew that this was where he belonged. The man's odour disgusted him and made the man seem even more menacing. The way the man held his penis proudly, as though grasping a spear in his fist, made Parker lean back and rest on his heels.

The man shuffled forward and reached for Parker and disturbed the wig.

'What's this supposed to be?'

And flung it down and saw Parker's short spiky hair and terrified eyes and clownish make-up – and he roared.

The strange man seemed to fill the room with his anger. There was fear as well as aggression in the way he slapped Parker's face and snatched at his clothes. He pulled Parker to an upright position and brought Parker's head down sharply on to the anvil of his knee – two or three times. Parker was stunned after the first one. He did not resist, did not even lift his arms to protect himself. He simply wanted it to be over. In his thrashing the man tipped the lamp over, and Parker went with it, and crushed it. Then the room was dark, and the man was angrier and began to kick him.

'You faggot, you bastard –'

They will hear, Parker thought. The man's shouts would rouse everyone in the building. He did not want anyone to see the man or to know any of this. He felt responsible for the man's rage and his humiliation, and he was glad when the man whinnied for breath and stumbled from the room. He left the house fast.

Twice, lying there, Parker thought he heard voices outside. But no one knocked, no one had woken, or, if they heard the struggle, no one inquired. Parker still lay where he fell, unable to rise. The pain did not subside; it was overtaken by another numbness, and he slept.

When he woke, he was ashamed, and he could only think of that man he had tricked. It was wrong to provoke a person into becoming a brute, simply because the man was a stranger. He hated the thought that he was inspiring violence in these men. He had had an obscure sense that they might finish him off: that was the only justice, it seemed. But look at the effect he had on them. It was not fair to make them rage at him. It was a perverse way of taking them down with him.

He was too bruised to go out again for a few days, perhaps more than a few. He had stopped counting the days, he never knew the time, he seldom ate. He wanted only to die, and so numbers had no meaning for him. Only the living cared about counting.

Once, he had thought how appropriate it would be for him to go out cruising at night and pick up a man and be killed. Now he saw the wrong in this, how his remorse had made him stupid. He had no right to turn a man into a killer. He deserved to die, but no one else must be involved in his death. He was the killer, so there was only one way. There had only been one way all along, and he had avoided it. The beating had weakened him. He needed another day to be strong enough to go through with it.

Parker woke and went to the mirror. He had no face, no reflection: he saw nothing. So the day had come.

Walking through the Loop he was glad no one saw the sad man he was. They saw a silly woman, and didn't care.

He remembered how a few blocks away, in June, he

180

had almost been killed – run down by a bus. He felt bitter that it had not happened then. But in a sense he had begun to die that day. That was the first day of his death, and this would be the last.

At this moment, as he walked down the broad sidewalk of Jackson, the police were looking for him – searching for Parker Jagoda and also searching for the killer they knew as The Wolfman. They had nothing on an ungainly blonde in a blue skirt and white blouse, with a scarf around her hair and partly covering her face; with big feet. He passed two policemen on the corner of North Franklin. They didn't see him.

Dressed as his victim, he had assumed – by pure fluke – the perfect disguise. Sharon was the one person on earth whom no one was looking for. He could have survived for years like this, undetected. But he had no right to do that – he had no rights at all, no murderer had.

The concourse area of the Sears Tower had the atmosphere of a state fair: excited crowds of people from out of town waiting their turn on the elevator as though it was a fair-ground ride. Office workers were returning from their lunch hour, and mingled with them and getting underfoot were groups of children – kids from summer camps, kids from clubs, kids in identical tee-shirts. They fussed and were noisy, and some of them rode with Parker on the ear-crackling elevator to the observation level.

Parker was dismayed by the way the windows were sealed, by the locks on the doors, by the watchful security guards. He went higher, to the antenna level – outside – and was almost blinded by the sight of the great blue lake and the brown horizontal city stretching into the sun. People screeched, because they were nervous at this height, and because it was very windy. The whine of the rising wind helped him think: it exactly matched the sound that was coursing through his brain.

He hung on to his wig, clutched at his clothes – but only for appearance's sake. He didn't want to attract attention. He walked the whole perimeter of the barrier, on which helpful notices were posted: *Do Not Attempt To* and *It Is Dangerous To* and *It Is An Offence To*. The signs attracted him and concentrated his attention, and helped him work out a precise plan.

'– *world's tallest building*,' a boasting commentary was braying out of a loudspeaker, while Parker lurked near the barrier.

A small girl frowned at him and came closer.

'Why are you crying?' she asked.

'Because I'm so happy to be up here in the Sears Tower,' Parker said.

She screwed up one eye and said, 'But why?'

'Because it's the one place in Chicago where you don't have to look at the Sears Tower,' he said.

The little girl wrinkled her nose at this and left him. And then he braced himself against the glass at the corner of the barrier and hoisted himself to the top, and swung his leg over this oversized fishtank. As he vaulted it – losing his wig, tearing his blouse – he heard a cry. Someone had seen him, but he was over. The glass muffled the commotion of the people pressing forward for a look.

The wind tore at him as he hurried to the parapet and climbed another guard rail to another barrier fence. The roofs projected outwards – he could see across but not down. He fought forward against the wind to the last fence, at the lip of the building, and he went light-headed at the sight of the miles of vacant air and the great distance down.

He thought of nothing except what he was about to do. Nothing existed on earth except him, and that was why he was superfluous. He had to go. He was an error that needed to be eliminated. He was no more than what he felt like here: an insignificant speck.

He began to strip off his clothes, tearing off his blouse, slipping off his skirt – and off with his underwear and socks. He had only to release them from his fingers for them to fill with air and fly and twist away.

Then he was naked, and eager to go, and as near to being truly happy as he had ever been. This was the only good deed he had ever done in his life. He looked back and saw two security men pursuing him, but they were fearful of the height, of the wind, of all the sharp obstructions on the jutting shelf. They were slow and came on cautiously; but Parker had no such fears.

He shrieked and jumped out eagerly and was snatched into the wind – his whole body was buffeted. He had a strong feeling that he had made a mistake: that he was not falling but being borne aloft, like his clothes, and soaring over Chicago; that he would go on living. His remorse left him, he was cleansed by the wind and so vitalized by a surge of hope he began to count. He was sure he was flying.